The Grinning Man

Lucid Dreams

By

JM Steiner

Chapter 1

My name is Chance Curran – Chance because I was a chance baby; not a mistake. And if there is one indisputable truth in my life, it's that I'm supposed to be dead.

But I'm getting ahead of myself.

Let's go back to the beginning...

My eyes lock onto the tacky cat clock ticking away above the numerous diplomas lining the wall before drifting down to the golden name plaque standing proudly for everyone to see the second they walk in.

Dr. Isolde Ashford.

I try to ignore the woman with her dirty blonde hair pulled in a ridiculously tight bun and writing in her notebook. I try to ignore the overly stuffed cushion under my ass. I try to ignore the feeling of icy blue eyes boring a hole in my head. My fingers pick at the skin on my arms, and as a headache forms and my mouth begins to hurt, I realize I need to unclench my teeth.

"Now, let's start from the top to make sure we didn't miss anything," she says. Her voice is smooth and low, possessing an almost hypnotizing edge that tempts me to listen. Instead, annoyance flares up, and my nails dig into my palms, almost to the point of drawing blood.

"I already told you everything," I spit out.

"Humor me."

I roll my eyes, steel my nerves, and exhale deeply.

"Fine. Let's do it then.

I was setting off for the 8 o'clock tour, and we had a full group; twelve in total with seven guys, four women, and a kid. She was about 15 or 16 – can't remember exactly. We were set to walk along the coast to hopefully spot some whales, walk the trails of the forest, hit a rest stop, stop in a clearing for the best view of the Northern lights, and head back to end the tour. Simple and easy. They asked a lot of questions.

"What type of whales pass through here?" one asked.

"B-Beluga."

"What typa bears are 'round here?" another asked, her Brooklyn accent strong.

"B-brown, black, grizzly, polar, and y-you can find Kodiak on the Kodiak Island."

"What time do the whales usually breach the surface?" a guy asked.

"I-it depends. They breach for a n-number of reasons like breathing, playing, tryna mate, o-or other reasons. It's pretty random."

"Why is it constantly dark? It's so depressing!" the kid asked.

"S-something about the Earth's axis?"

"Do you have to stutter through everything? And why are you so weird? Aren't tour guides supposed to be charming or something?" the kid scoffed. The kid was kinda a dick throughout the whole trip, to be honest.

I tried to usher them along as fast as possible when I noticed the kid's weird behavior from the corner of my eye. She kept crossing her arms over her chest, tugging at her hair, and looking over her shoulder. The others in the group hadn't noticed, too busy asking questions, and I really didn't want to be the one to bring it up. After the tenth time and her steadily moving closer to me, though, I finally said something.

"I-is there something wrong?"

She scoffed and tried to look annoyed, but her constant shifting gave her away.

"Yeah, apparently some dude was late to the tour and is just now trying to join. Looks drunk, too, 'cause he's acting like a total freak," she spat. Almost as a unit, everyone turns to look behind us, and we all see the same thing.

A guy was about a yard away, and it looked like he was looking up towards the sky. His body swayed so erratically that I thought he was about to fall to the side. Hell, I was waiting for it. Instead, he just progressively moved closer as his arms swung in a weird way around him. Everyone started muttering to themselves about it, and I just cupped my hands around my mouth.

"Hey! I-I'm sorry, sir, but the group's full!"

He made no indication that he heard me and still moved forward.

Everyone soon started to look a bit concerned and a few heads turned my way. I ran my fingers through my hair a couple of times and tried to ignore the stares. I kept calling out to him to stop him but nothing worked, and the group grew more uneasy as the man was now about four yards away.

"I-I said w-we're full!"

"He obviously ain't listening," Brooklyn asked. I take a glance around me, square my shoulders, and I start to approach him. My blood started to pump furiously as I got closer and *stopped when I was a good distance away from the man; close enough to try and intimidate him but far enough to turn tail and run.*

"D-did you hear me? W-we're full!"

I took a few steps back when the man stopped moving – dancing, really, now that I was closer – and came to a complete standstill. It startled me enough that I took another step back. He stood still for a full three minutes, and I could vaguely hear the group saying something to me.

After that…"

"After that?" Isolde prompts. I shake my head, and my eyes close tightly. *Blood and screams* fill my mind, and my hands clutch my ears, my body scrunching into itself. Something is missing in my head; a few blank spots coating my mind, concealing whatever pieces of memories should be there. A fresh wave of anxiety crashes over me, and I can only ride it out. After a moment of harsh breathing and a nauseous sensation deep in my stomach, it's finally over and I can make out the sounds of a pencil scratching against paper.

"Chance, what you're experiencing has a very simple term. You see, you've developed false memories. It's a psychological phenomenon where an individual recalls an occurrence substantially differently from how it actually transpired or even an event that never happened," she explains. Her hands are folded together, and she looks the epitome of condescension. "There was no trace of a 'dancing man;' everything points to an animal being the culprit."

I couldn't stop the scowl from forming even if I tried, and I gotta admit that I wasn't really fighting it.

"I can't remember clearly, but I know for a fact that it wasn't an animal."

"Yes, it was. An animal attacked the group, most likely a polar bear a little far from home, and you were lucky enough to survive the ordeal. Your mind is refusing to remember the trauma and is now making up events to fill in the blank places. In addition to that, you are suffering from survivor's guilt and need a human to blame. Someone capable of doing harm and being aware of it as opposed to an animal just being an animal. You want an enemy, Chance," Isolde recounts. I clench my teeth and lean back in my seat, my legs spreading.

"So, you're saying I made this terrifying man up to make myself feel better?"

"Not exactly," she says. She stands and comes around to the front of the desk, resting half of her ass on the edge. Her long legs crossed together, and all I could think about was the fact that her short pencil skirt and unbuttoned white dress shirt, revealing traces of her lacy black bra, made her look like she was about to star in some poorly written fanfic that was 90% awkward sex and created by some teenage virgin.

"Then what?"

"I'm saying you needed someone who wasn't there, so you created him there."

"I feel like you're just repeating crap with a fancy college twist."

"I'm just trying to help you understand," she sighs. She leans forward and places a hand on my thigh, and I can feel the muscle tensing beneath it.

"Whatever."

Things are silent for a moment, and I watch as a million thoughts shift behind her eyes. I think about what she wants to tell me but keep coming up blank.

That seems to be the new default.

"You know, you left your shirt back at my place, along with a few other things. When are you coming back around to get it?" I cringe a little at her words and start picking at my skin again.

"Just drop it off at my place."

"Would it be okay if I spent the night?" When I don't answer, she slowly walks towards me and kneels between my spread legs. Her hands gently caress my knees, and she's looking up at me through long eyelashes. I quickly knock her hands off me, ignore her expression, and stand up, forcing her to move away.

"No. Is that all?"

Isolde clears her throat a couple of times, blinks a few times more than necessary, and fixes her already perfect hair.

"Yes, I-I mean no. You should also know that I'm also going to be increasing your Latuda," she says. I feel my face scrunch a bit, and my eyes cut to her.

Great. As if the current dosage wasn't bad enough. Whatever. It might help out.

I just nod and try to ignore her as she starts walking beside me. Her hand brushes against mine, so I shove both of mine in my pockets. I hear a soft sigh, and she opens the door, letting me walk out. I go to the front desk to sign out and set my sights on the ginger behind the desk.

She has wild, curly red hair that dances as she bobs her head to some song I can hear from here. My feet drag across the dark wooden floor until I stand in front of her, waiting for her to notice me, so I can leave. Instead, the girl – *Sibyl*, as her nametag says – keeps lip-synching, and I knock on the desk. Deep green eyes snap in my direction, and her mouth slightly drops open. Before I know it, she yanks her headphones out and smiles big.

"Hey! I literally didn't see you there! I was listening to that new Star ☆Girl song, y'know, the one about underwater UFO? Did you see the music video for it? Victor Brandon is so hot and is literally the best dancer in the world! Oh!" She suddenly leans in a bit too close, and I lean back, trying to hide my grimace. "Did you hear that they might be having an affair? I mean, it's probably true since she has him in *every* one of her videos. Must suck for his wife. I mean, having to watch your man dancing with one of the hottest singers while you're stuck at home with three kids? Couldn't be me."

"I-I, y-yeah, I guess. Could you just let me sign out?"

"Oh! Yeah, of course!"

She slides me the sheet, and I hurry to sign it and pay the bill. Her eyes scan the sheet before widening, a soft gasp leaving her lips. She looks up at me and begins to pretty much buzz in her seat. I pick at my arms, wishing she would just hurry up with the receipt, but she doesn't take her eyes off me.

"I didn't know that was you!"

"What do you mean?"

"You know! You're that tour guide whose entire group literally died that night! Is it true that it was an animal attack or was it, like, an actual person?" My stomach drops as she says this, and I look around the room, ignoring the gaze burning into the side of my head.

"Can you just print out my bill, please?"

"Yeah, yeah! You must be going crazy with all the gossip going around," Sibyl Adler says. Her orange-red curls bounce as she types on the computer. "I literally couldn't deal if everyone thought I was a killer."

When she holds out the receipt, I snatch it quickly and walk quickly to the door.

"Rude."

****

Home sweet home.

I'm sitting in my crappy Jeep Wrangler when I catch my reflection in the rear-view mirror. My usual tanned complexion looks a lot paler; my blue eyes look darker and more sunken than usual, with heavy, dark bags under those eyes, and my usually curly, light brown hair now hangs limply over my forehead. All-in-all, I look like I have one foot in the grave and am boldly circling the drain.

I look exactly like the psycho that everyone claims I am.

After noticing I've been sitting here for an hour, I finally get out and head inside the small, pale-blue, 2-story home with nothing around it but woods and silence.

Chapter 2

Trees passed by me and my arms pumped at my side as I took glances behind me. I had no idea what I was running from, but whatever it was, it had me scared enough to have sweat pouring down my face, my heart in my stomach, and my blood running cold, a chill running down my spine. Thin branches whipped against my face and left behind bleeding cuts and welts.

I continued to run in some unknown direction before something harshly struck my back and sent me careening down a steep incline. Dirt kicked up and choked me before I finally landed. I rolled on my back, chest heaving, but a heavy weight dropped on my stomach. My eyes snapped open, but my vision was blurred through tears.

My mouth dropped open, and I screamed.

Shooting up, I struggle to catch my breath and throw the covers from my body. I wipe my drenched face and bury it in my hands, trying to collect myself.

What the hell was that? Why did I dream that?

I look out the window before scoffing and looking at my phone— stupid 24-hour cycle. I turn on the screen, take a moment to look at the lock screen picture of a small boy sitting on the shoulders of an older teen, and finally look at the time.

2:09.

Fuck, did I seriously sleep for that long? Whatever. Better do something productive.

I get up and trip over some clothes on my way out of the room. As I'm walking through the halls on the top floor, I look at the few family photos on the wall, only to bang my hip on an end table. I spit out a curse and then push the table further against the wall, chipping off some of the pale blue paint that I've never bothered to change over the years. My phone vibrates in my sweatpants pocket, and I pull it out and check the notifications.

"For fuck's sake, Isolde," I mutter.

I walk inside the kitchen, scratching at my bare chest, and think about my plans for today. I need to go job hunting soon before my funds run out. Plus, I need to do some work around the house. It would've been easier if I could just hire someone to do it but…

Who the hell would want to go in a murderer's house?

I sigh heavily and try to think happier thoughts. Like, what should I eat for breakfast? French toast?

I'm kinda not in the mood for bread.

Cereal?

Nah, I don't want anything cold.

"Eggs and bacon it is."

However, the only thing that greets me is two half-empty bottles of cheap bourbon, a few slices of American cheese, an old Chinese takeout box that I don't remember ordering, and a container of cottage cheese I can smell from here.

Great.

After a glance around the room, I see a dark green shirt on the floor and throw it on since it's clean enough before heading out, keys in hand.

****

Some crappy song is playing on the radio, and I take the moment to just lose myself. My place is about 30 minutes away from town, something that my brother used to love just for the sole reason of being able to play his drums as loud as he wanted— used to drive my parents crazy.

I barely catch sight of some moose grazing on the grass when I spot a lone black dog running across the grasslands. It gets closer to the small herd, and just when I think it's going to run into the herd and most likely attack, it disappears. I keep looking, expecting to see it run from the herd or attack one of them, but nothing happens. The moose didn't even react like there wasn't a predator nearby.

The car vibrates harshly as it hits the rumble strips, and I turn my attention back to the road and pull the car back on the road. I can't help but glance a couple of times at the moose, and they're still eating.

That's freaky.

Whatever the case, I continue the drive to the market. As I park my car and get out, I notice a group of goth teens skateboarding and messing around. One of them, a female with a bad dark red dye job, points in my direction, and they all look at me. The one that stands out the most is a short male with black hair, pale skin, and, just like the others, wearing all black. He's sitting on his skateboard and glaring hard at me, completely motionless. I notice the others around him saying something, but he doesn't respond.

Freaky ass kid.

I walk quicker to the entrance, grab a cart, and begin my shopping. Quicks-Bee is the only decent store around here and given the fact that most of the stuff they sell here is frozen meals, junk food, and cheap booze, that's saying a lot about this town. I immediately go to the produce aisle, and the light spray of vapor hits me. Out of the corner of my eye, I can see some people standing nearby, but I keep on doing what I'm doing.

"... what happened last night?"

"... a murder... Witch Pine Forest..."

"How the hell isn't he in jail right now?"

"... police connections..."

If that's their version of whispering, they must've been hated in high school. As I'm picking up some green peppers, I spot three chicks about my age huddling together and taking glances at me. When I look in their direction, they stare hard at me, and the one in the middle scoffs and crosses her arms over her chest.

"Wanna know what I heard?" she asks. Her voice was louder than before, and she kept eye contact with me. "I heard that the bodies were completely mutilated. Their limbs were torn off, their guts were spilling, and some of them were even missing their heads."

"Eww gross! Are you serious?" the short brunette asks. Her face is pale, and she looks like she's about to throw up.

"Just like that tour incident," the chick with dyed pink hair says.

"Yup. Some people believe that it was an animal, but…" the blonde says. She looks at me harder, and I start to squirm, picking at my arms and trying to avoid her gaze. "I don't think that. I think the real killer was a sick, psychotic freak."

Soft whimpers. Screeching pleads. Sickening squelching. Silent prayers.

My head starts to pound, and I throw the green peppers in the cart, not caring what happens to them. I push my cart away, ignoring the smug expression on the blonde and the disgusted one on the brunette and try to hurry, so I can leave.

Fuck this small-town mentality. Why doesn't anyone see things from my perspective? I tried to help those people, I tried telling the police that there was a man who did it, but no one listened! I'm the only witness; the sole survivor-

You don't deserve it.

So, why won't they take my word for it? Do they honestly think that I'm strong enough to kill an entire group? That I'm sick enough to try?

Maybe you are.

I wouldn't hurt anyone, and if I did, I would remember it. I would remember dismembering a body, murdering a bunch of innocent people – *including a kid* – I would remember everything, but I don't!

Tossing milk, cereal, and other items in the cart, I notice that more and more people are watching me. I wish there was a hole that I could bury myself in, and I'm sure that's a shared sentiment. I finally get to an empty lane which is run by a tall, lanky guy probably in his mid-20s. I put the items on the belt and wait for him to do his job.

The guy keeps taking glances at me as he scans the items, and I start tapping some random rhythm on the belt.

"Did you find everything you need, sir?"

"Y-yeah, thank you," I mutter.

"Good, good."

An awkward silence takes over.

"So, you're a tour guide, right?" I side-eye him before nodding slightly.

"Y-yeah, so?"

"You know a lot about the bears? Like how aggressive they are?"

"Yeah, t-the polar bears are the most aggressive although grizzlies with attack if y-you get too close to their territory o-or cubs."

He scans a bit slower and nods his head.

"So pretty much aggressive enough to kill humans?"

"Yeah, mostly likely t-the polar bears though. They're not afraid to hunt and eat them."

"In other words, it's entirely possible for polar bears to kill… I don't know, an entire tour group? Or is that complete bull?" He bags the items even slower as my stomach plummets.

Why can't they just leave me alone?

With that, I hurry up to pay, take my bags, and rush out of the store. I look towards the ground as the same group of girls from before watching me leave. I keep my eyes down and fumble to get my keys out. When I finally look up, the keys slip from my hand along with one of the bags.

My car was completely fucked.

The tires are slashed, the windshield is shattered, but the biggest damage is what's spray-painted right on the side in black.

MURDERER

My eyes start to burn, and I blink rapidly and pick and scratch at my arms. I swallow harshly and drop to the ground to pick my groceries back up. A pair of black vans stop in front of me, and I focus on the mixed-matched laces; the right shoe has light blue laces while the left one has dark purple.

I flinch when the light blue laced shoe presses on my fingers and begins applying pressure. I quickly pull my hand to my chest, managing to keep the damage to a slight throbbing sensation, but keep my eyes on those laces.

"You're so fucking pathetic, dude," he says. One of his friends lets out a short laugh in disbelief, prompting the others to start laughing under their breaths.

The boy's voice is still in the process of puberty, but I'm pretty sure he wouldn't appreciate me pointing out the slight break in his voice. Besides, it didn't take away from the venom in his tone.

"I can't believe that all those people died by someone like *you*."

"T-they d-d-didn't," I tell him. Unfortunately, it comes out as a pathetic whimper that leads to the group laughing again; louder and more mocking.

"T-they d-didn't! I-I'm i-innocent!" the teen mocks before lunging at me, causing me to fall back. "Save that bullshit for your psychiatrist, you fucking nutcase! You did it! You killed all those people, but you're getting a get-out-of-jail-free pass just because you're fucked in the head!"

"I don't see why they don't put him in an asylum," one of the other guys says.

"Skip the asylum, just fry his ass."

"Maybe lethal injection? I heard they botch those a lot."

"Or the firing squad. I think they still do that."

They started laughing harder as they surrounded me, discussing different ways for me to die. I don't even know when I got to my feet, but I do know that I hunched in on myself and tried to block out their words, just standing there and taking it.

He spits at my feet, shoulders me as he goes by, and leads them away.

I leave the smashed produce on the ground but pick up everything else, struggling not to drop anything. It's hard to open the back door, but when I do, I place them carelessly on the floor. I slam the door shut, and the fragile glass shatters. I get in the driver's seat, softly close the door, and can only fall in a daze as I stare at the steering wheel.

A wave of negative emotions crashes down on me, and I bite my lip hard, trying to stifle everything down. My body feels like it's vibrating, and I begin to beat on the wheel.

BEEP

BEEP

BEEP

BEEP

"FUCK! FUCK, FUCK, FUCK, FUCK, FUCK, FUCK, FUCK!"

Sobs fill the open air, and I can't barely catch my breath. The walls feel like they're closing in on me, and I start to feel lightheaded. It's hard to swallow past the lump in my throat, and I can't stop sniffling. It takes a few minutes before I wipe my face. When my vision clears, I look up and something catches my eye from the rearview mirror— something swaying. I whip around and see a tall man sitting straight, the top of his head pressing against the roof of the car.

I instantly recognize the wide, painful grin of the man from the tour, and I exhale softly.

"This can't be real."

The man doesn't move, doesn't blink, doesn't breathe, and we're locked in each other's gaze. Now that I can see him closer, I can see that he's wearing a pressed dark blue suit, a dark-colored tie, maybe black or navy blue, and a white dress shirt buttoned up to his neck.

"This can't be real," I mutter and turn back around. My hand struggles to pop open the glove department, and when it does, multiple pill bottles spill to the floor. I can see his body slightly shifting from the corner of my eye, and his arm lifts, pointing to the side. He's pointing at something outside – what? I don't know.

I finally find one with a few still in there and swallow two of them dry. He doesn't disappear, but I can't focus on that. Instead, I focus on riding back on the rims of my slashed tires.

Chapter 3

I don't know why, but I was jogging down the sidewalk. It was still dark out due to the night cycle, so I couldn't even tell what time it was. The air was crisp and fresh, and it tasted refreshing. It made my workout more enjoyable, and the lull that hung over everything created a peaceful atmosphere.

Despite this, it felt like something was brewing beneath the surface; a beast lying in wait, ready to pounce. I couldn't quite put my finger on what was wrong, but the feeling was there. With that in mind, I started to jog faster, probably wanting to go home.

I couldn't help but keep looking over my shoulder expecting to find the source of my unease but see nothing. It wasn't until I caught a glimpse in my peripheral that I noticed the figure walking on the opposite sidewalk. I looked up and saw a tall man who was wearing a suit and moving strangely. He moved as if he was waltzing, but something else seemed wrong with his silhouette.

When he passed by under a streetlight, I finally realized that his head was tilted back, the back of his head almost touched his shoulders and his neck strained with the pose. When he was further ahead of me, I realized that I had started to slow down. My heart pounded in my head when I made eye contact with him, and I felt a violent shudder run through me.

It was time to go, so I turned on my heels and started heading back. I was too tired to run or jog back, but the weird man's presence did put some pep in my step.

As I walked, I would make sure to keep looking over my shoulder to keep an eye on him. At first, I was able to see him until I stumbled over an uneven portion of the sidewalk.

A minute.

I only took my eyes off of him for a minute, and the next time I looked up, he was gone. A grimace formed on my face, and I turned my head back around.

Things were already pretty quiet before, but there was at least the soft chirping of crickets and the soft sounds of owls hooting.

Now? Absolutely nothing.

I must've walked for another 20 minutes before I started hearing soft but rapid footsteps behind me. A feeling of shame swelled when my head refused to even look back as I desperately prayed that it would go away if I didn't see it. Like I was a fucking kid who still hid under the covers from the monster in the closet.

It wasn't until I could hear the deep, steady breathing and felt a cold puff of air hit the back of my head that I realized whoever it was had caught up. Another violent shudder wrecked my body, and I forced my body forward and spun to confront him. My entire body tensed when I came face-to-face with the man. His eyes were bloodshot wide and that grin still strained his face.

Worse... his head was still tilted back, and I realized he had been running at me backward.

"G-g-get the hell away from me, you freak!"

"I beg your pardon, where are my manners? Allow me to introduce myself; you may call me Cold. It's a pleasure to meet you, Mr. Curran."

He was talking to me. His mouth hadn't moved, always stayed with that mouth-splitting mouth, but he talked to me. His voice was clear and was neither deep nor high, and it held an accent that he couldn't place with strange inflections at random moments in his sentences.

"This can't be happening. Stay the hell away from me!" I tried to move back, but my feet were glued in place.

"No need for all of that, Mr. Curran. I have not come to hurt you; I just need a moment of your time. What I have to tell you is the difference between your life and death."

Wake up, Chance. Wake up, wake up, wake up, wake the fuck up!

The first thing that I see is that familiar ceiling, and I can't help but choke out a sob. It was just a dream… a very, very fucked dream. Though, even as the scenes flash through my mind, why does it still feel like I'm missing something? I rub my hands down my face and take a deep breath.

I drag myself out of bed with only the thoughts of a routine in mind. Take a piss, wash my hands, brush my teeth, take my pills, and *breathe*. Ignore, ignore, ignore – don't focus on the window; don't focus on the forest. Then, on to the next routine: pick up dirty clothes and bedding and toss them in the washing machine, *no point in separating colors*, make some breakfast- some cheap knockoff of Frosted Flakes- and clean up around the place.

As I start dusting, I prop open the window before lighting up a cigarette. Smoke fills my lungs as I inhale softly then I exhale from the side of my mouth. The brisk air hits my face, and it sends a pleasurable chill down my spine. I dust at the windowsill when some black, flying thing comes through.

"What the hell?"

I try to swat it out, but it lands on the windowsill, wings fluttering gently.

Is that… a butterfly? I didn't even know they came in this shade.

Sure enough, after closer inspection, I can see that this is a black butterfly. It moves gently along the sill, closer to me, and something compels me to hold my hand out. It's only then that I see claw marks running deep in the wood of the windowsill. The butterfly seems to avoid the marks, but I run my finger down it.

"What the hell did this? And what was it trying to do? Trying to climb inside?" With that in mind, I can't imagine some dog or something climbing up the side of my house. I planted blackberry bushes under all of the windows, and the thorns should prevent anything from getting too close. I even planted some Alaskan Monkshoods as a further deterrent.

In other words, no living creature should even attempt to get close to my house.

Putting the marks in the back of my mind, I look back to the butterfly. It moves up my hand, and a chill runs down my spine. A lone, bass-heavy howl calls from the forest, startling me and sending the butterfly flying.

"Maybe I need more bushes."

❊❊❊❊❊❊❊❊❊❊❊❊❊

"It's $263 for the windshield, $237 for the backdoors, each, $730 for all the tires, and $530 to get out all of those scratches since they were so deep," the voice on the other line drawls. I run a hand through my hair as I lean against the counter.

"Are you serious?"

"Look, man, whoever did this to the car was on some Street Fighter shit, and it's gonna cost some cash to fix it. We have a pretty good rental service."

I groan softly. *How the hell am I going to get by these next couple of months?*

I've been on the phone for what seems like hours talking with this guy that I'm pretty sure is jacking up the prices out of spite. I'm already barely making it by; I've not been back to work since the attack, and I only have a little over 3,000 in my bank. This car is going to fuck me over, and I still gotta worry about bills, groceries, and anything else I might need before I find another job.

"O-okay, fine, fine, fine; I'll do the rental services."

"Great. We'll have it delivered to your address, free of charge. Consider it a gift. Have a nice day," he says sarcastically. He hangs up before I can say anything, but, really, what could I even say? Just when I think my day couldn't get any worse, a call comes in with a familiar ID.

"What do you want, Isolde? I'm not in the mood."

"Calm down, this is for business, not pleasure. I want to hear your progress. Is everything good with the medication? No new side effects?"

My mind goes back to the Grinning Man and the nightmares. *He isn't there, Chance, you're just imagining him, remember?* God, I can hear her practically licking her chops at the notion, just waiting to throw some more psychiatry bull my way.

"Nope, nothing new."

"That's great! What about your nightmares? I remember you once saying something about strange dreams. Are you still experiencing them?"

"No, no weird dreams. Hell, I've been sleeping so deep lately, I don't even remember my dreams." Maybe it was the slight crack in my voice, maybe it was her intuition, or maybe she just knows me too well, but silence falls over us.

"Is that the truth?"

"Of course it is."

"Chance, I can't help you if you don't help me."

As much as I hated to admit it – and I hated to – maybe she was right. Maybe her psychiatry bullshit is what I need to help understand those nightmares or even bring me a step closer to remembering something.

"Okay, fine. I'm still having the dreams," I say. A heavy sigh leaves my lips, and I pick at the skin on the tip of my fingers. "I think they're getting worse. At first, it was just me feeling this-this *deep* sense of dread, but I always woke up pretty quickly. Now, I'm always running from something, running from that Grinning Man. I always wake up, feeling like I'm missing something, and it's driving me… *insane*."

And that was it, wasn't it? I'm going insane, I have to be. There's no other logical explanation. I just feel like a contradiction: I believe that this man is real and is trying to kill me to tie up loose ends, but I also know for an undeniable fact that he's a figment of my imagination and I'm losing my fucking mind. I don't want to go crazy, I *fear* it, but it seems inevitable.

"Chance, this is normal. It's progress! We know that there's no Grinning Man, *you* know there's no Grinning Man. You keep trying to block out the truth, you keep running from it, but your subconscious wants to reveal it. I bet that if you let the *Grinning Man* catch up with you, it will reveal the truth," she says. There's a short pause, and my heart does pick up during that time.

But he did catch up with me.

"It will reveal that he's not real, Chance. Talk to him. *Confront* him. The more you run, the more you repress your memories and bury the truth."

And there it was. The confirmation that I was looking for, that I was suspecting, and yet it doesn't feel good. It feels like a bitter pill to swallow, and I nod even though she can't see.

"Well, isn't that great to hear?"

"Look, i-if you're that stressed about this and need someone to talk to, I have no problem seeing you outside of our sessions. It doesn't even have to be about the dreams. W-we can just distract ourselves and watch some movies with some takeout or something," she pauses and breathes out deeply. "I'm sorry, I don't know why I said that."

"Neither do I. Listen, I gotta go-"

"Just wait a minute, Chance. I'm sorry, I won't bring it up." She sighs, and I briefly find humor in the fact that she seems to be doing that a lot around me. For whatever reason, I don't hang up. "I just want to give you a sense of normalcy because that's what you need. Dealing with PTSD is hard as is but throwing Schizophrenia into the mix just makes it all the worse."

"Gee, because I didn't feel like a psycho freak already."

"I know none of this sounds ideal, but-"

"It's a process," we say. She sighs so softly that I almost miss it.

"Chance, you're not alone in this. I'm not just saying this as your psychiatrist; I'm saying this as your friend and as someone who cares deeply about you."

Gratification swells inside of me, and I can't stop the small smile from slipping on my lips. I pull the phone a little closer and stare out the nearby window.

"Thanks, Izzy."

"It's no problem, Chance. I'm always here for you," she says. There it was again; that expectant tone. "Always."

"Goodbye, Isolde." Without waiting for her to respond, I hung up the phone.

I'm feeling pretty claustrophobic. A walk around town and some fresh air sounds like a good idea. Hopefully, I won't run into those little gothic shits again.

****

I just want it to be on record that I usually have better ideas than this.

Honestly, I was enjoying my walk at first; the air tasted fresh, the air felt cool against my skin, and the general mood was just washing my thoughts away. But like I said, that was at first. Now? I lower my head as yet another person gestures in my direction, talking to their friend. They both look at me before hurrying along. It doesn't take me long to figure out the reason why.

"There was another attack, and the murderer is just walking free."

"They're never going to end until he's locked up."

"Or until someone kills him."

There they go again. It's funny… They want me dead because they believe I killed people despite being proven innocent, so they essentially want the death of an innocent man. Instead of paying any more attention to them, I just pull the hood of my jacket over my head and move quickly.

Before I can do anything or even process what's happening, someone pulls me into the alleyway and slams me against the wall. The impact is harsh enough to knock the breath out of me as my spine hits the brick wall, and my head collides with it even harder. Tears instinctively swell in my eyes, but the large hand tightly gripping the collar of my shirt and cutting off my air feels like a bigger priority.

I force my eyes open, and the first thing that I see is light brown eyes glaring down resentfully at me.

Chapter 4

"W-what-"

"You think you're tough shit, huh?"

"I-I-I-I d-d-don't-!"

I'm cut off as he slams me against the wall again, and I cough harshly when he tightens his grip on my shirt. He moves his face closer until I can see every one of his features up close.

"I know what you did, jack-off!"

"F-f-for the last time, I didn't kill those people!"

A deep growl rumbles from his chest, and it reminds me of a rabid dog. The thought has my lip twitching which turns out to be a mistake. His pupils seem to blow wide so much that they almost blacken his entire eyes, giving him a demonic look.

And that's when the first punch is thrown.

It whips across my jaw and disorients me. I swear I hear a click, and I have to wiggle it around a couple of times to make sure no bones are broken. Almost immediately, he starts raining punches down my face before throwing me to the ground. I hit some trash bins and one of the busted-up ones cut my forehead with the sharp metal. A combination of that and his heavy hits soon had blood gushing down my face and blinding my right eye.

Now, all I can do is cover my head and try to defend myself as he starts to kick and stomp me repeatedly. He suddenly moves me to my back, straddles my body, and starts brutally punching my nose. The beating is relentless and ruthless with raw power backing every punch.

I can feel the rage and disgust pouring out of him in waves, overwhelming me to the point where it feels like I have to throw up- from either that or the concussion I most definitely have.

"Stay away from my brother."

With that, he punctuates the warning with one final punch that snaps my head back and everything goes black.

I was in the woods again, hidden in some bushes. I was crouched in an uncomfortable position, but something told me not to move. It seemed like whenever I was in these dreams, visions? Memories? I always had these intuitions about what to do or where to go. While helpful, it also filled me with dread.

Why the hell would I know this?

I shifted a bit in place and tentatively pushed aside an opening to get a clue about what I was dealing with.

My gasp was too audible in my ears, and I pressed my hands hard against my mouth and, subsequently, my nose. I hadn't even realized it until I started having difficulties breathing. In my haste, I had moved back, and my heart pounded in my chest. I swallowed harshly, closed my eyes, and tried to get myself back in the right mindset.

Then I moved back.

I had gathered as much courage as I could at that moment and saw exactly what I had expected at that point – that damn man again. Doing the same damn thing; waltzing in the familiar drunken manner. His head was, again, almost perfectly perpendicular to the ground.

I wanted to look away – to move away before he discovered me. But, I also wanted to find out more clues about him. Every time I saw him, all he would do was either chase me or dance; there had to be something more with him.

I scanned his pristine suit, and, as if I now had hyper focus and vision, and I spotted his hands or, more specifically, his fingers. His nails had dirt caked under them. Not only that but said nails were broken as if he had clawed desperately at a hard surface. They were a sharp contrast against his otherwise clean appearance.

Why was that? What happened? What else could I find? Do I have to get closer just to get more clues?

That last one had sent a slight chill down my spine, and I figured that was a sign to get away while I still could.

Right as I was about to move away, I locked eyes with him.

****

This is becoming way too common.

That's the first thought in my mind as my eyes snap open, and I see a familiar chubby figure leaning over me, ginger curls brushing against my face (which hurts like a bitch – no doubt bruised to hell) and large dark green eyes blink once. I groan and attempt to push her face away, but my arm groans in protest the second I raise it.

"You should be more careful. You legit got your ass beat!"

"Thank you, Sibyl, I couldn't tell," I groan out.

It's only then that I realize I'm lying on the grimy ground of the same alleyway I was beaten in. I look around and see the trash bins I was thrown on now have blood splatters and noticeable dents. Not only the bins but the ground was also painted with blood, especially a particular large spot where my head was. I gently touch my head, but it's still too rough causing me to flinch in pain. I try again and run my fingers over some cotton-like fabric.

"An old shirt I found in the back of my car. Don't worry about returning it; it's flannel. I went through kind of a phase that I don't wanna talk about."

"…Okay?"

"Y'know, you have the worst luck! I mean, Austin knocked you around. Everyone in town is, like, talking about it. I was surprised that you were still here and that no one bothered picking you up. Like, *no one*."

"Okay, okay, I get it! I'm guessing the guy who beat me like I owed him money was Austin?"

She nodded a little too cheerfully for me and seemingly gazes into the distance, a soft sigh leaving her lips. I furrow my brows, follow her line of sight before looking back at her, and scoff a bit under my breath.

No fucking way.

"Yeah, Austin Haze. 6 ft 2 inches, 179 lbs. of lean, defined muscles, curly blonde hair that looks like it was perfectly styled by some angels, eyes like melted chocolate, a beautiful tan which is weird since he does ice hockey, and dimples whenever he flashes a smile. Not to mention a 4.2 GPA, captain of said ice hockey team, *and* a member of the *Omega Nu Delta* fraternity; the guy couldn't get any more perfect! You're so lucky that you got to get up close and personal with him!"

"Yeah, it was real personal when he was beating my face in," I said. A metallic, coopery taste fills my mouth, and I spit out a glob of blood. I roll to my side and after straining sore muscles and accidentally applying pressure to still-forming bruises, I finally manage to sit up. Sibyl helps me but presses a little too hard on my side.

"I'm not surprised he beat you so hard. Y'know, considering what happened and everything," she says.

"I have a massive headache which, I'm pretty sure, is veering into severe concussion territory. Can you please just tell me what you know?" She pouts and rolls her eyes.

"You're no fun. Whatever! Anyway, his dad was in the tour group that got killed during that incident. He has a younger brother who's in the same grade as my sister, but I forgot his name," she carelessly says.

All I can do is close my eyes and start laughing.

I don't know why I do, I don't know why I can't stop, but Sibyl is staring at me as if I am crazy. My cheeks start to feel cold, and when I rub them, I feel the wetness on them.

Fuck, I don't even know if it's from the blood or I'm just crying. All I know is that either blood or tears won't stop flowing.

"What's wrong with you?"

I shake my head and try to stop my shuddering breath. I should go home; I need to go home.

"Wait, Chance! Where the heck are you going?"

I just keep walking, allowing the fog to cloud my mind.

✱✱✱✱✱✱✱✱✱✱✱✱

It's a long trek home, and my focus and vision would blank in and out on multiple occasions.

When I get there, I see a familiar car in the driveway, and my already raging headache pounds even harder at the sight of the 73' cherry-red Pontiac Grand Am. And standing near it is a casually dressed Isolde. She's wearing a pair of skin-tight khaki jeans, a dark green long-sleeve shirt, brown boots, and an oversized dark brown, cable knit, cardigan sweater. Her long hair is hanging down one shoulder, and she pushes some locks that fall in front of her eyes.

Almost immediately, her hands are all over me, and I wince when she manages to touch every sore spot on my face. Sorrow fills her eyes before she gently cups my face.

"Chance, I heard about what happened! What the hell? We need to call the cops!" I gently move her hands away and take a step back, holding up my hand when she tries to follow.

"It's fine, Izzy. I just want to take a shower and go to sleep."

"What? What about the guy who assaulted you?"

"It doesn't matter. It's done and over with; just let it go," I say.

Honestly, I appreciate the concern, but I just want to forget this whole day. It just feels like one shitty event after another with zero breaks in between. I'm a social pariah, and the only person in my corner is Isolde.

But is she? She doesn't even believe you.

"You want to forget being attacked in broad daylight in front of who knows how many witnesses and have no one help?" For some reason, the words sound even harsher coming from her mouth, and it leaves a bitter taste in my mouth. "Chance, answer me! Why won't you get-"

"Fuck, Isolde! J-just-!" My hands don't know where to go, and I decide to settle them on my hips. "Just, please, *go*. I said I didn't want to call anyone, so why can't you just fucking drop it? I can't deal with the constant shit this town loves to throw my way, the constant beatings and harassment, the nightmares, the paranoia, waking up in a cold sweat, and, the cherry on this shit sundae, you constantly refuse to listen to anything I have to say; I'm done! I'm so fucking done!"

Isolde goes quiet and stares blankly at me, her gaze almost going through me. The air quickly becomes heavy, and I search her face for something, anything, that could tell me what she's feeling.

"I just want to help you, that's all I ever want to do. Chance, you're sick. I'm trying to stick by you, and you treat me like I'm the villain."

"Gee, you keep talking like that, I wonder why? Stop talking to me like I'm fucking crazy! The only thing I'm sick of is the constant shit I have to go through every day just because none of you in this fucked up town believes me when I explicitly tell you that I *saw* someone kill all of those people!"

She flinches, and I just notice how close I am to her now. Regret swells up inside, and I immediately walk backward until she grabs my hand. She looks up at me, and I exhale deeply, rubbing the back of my head with my free hand and thinking about how to proceed.

"Look, Isolde, I-I'm just not in the mood. Please, please, just… just go."

Isolde looks at me in a daze, and I just move her to the side to unlock my door. I just want to get in my house and lay in my bed. I faintly hear her say something, but the door soon blocks out whatever it is. I lean against it for a moment and just close my eyes. There's some faint knocking, and I can faintly hear her brush against the door.

"Okay, Chance. Don't forget I'm just a call away."

I don't respond, and I can soon hear her drive away, leaving me alone yet again.

Chapter 5

We rode on a tour bus going down that familiar route.

A man sat beside me with a large, easygoing grin on his face. He was tall and well-built with long, shaggy honey-blonde hair that had soft waves and fell to his shoulders, dark gray eyes that held so much warmth behind them, and crinkles appeared around those eyes when he gave people that dimpled smile. His whole person was just vibrant, and you could tell by the way everyone's eyes would drift to him every minute.

I hunched in my seat and mentally prepared for all of the possible talking points when the man started to talk to me.

"So, how old are you, kid?" His voice is deep but, like the rest of him, friendly enough. I took a couple of glances at him and remained silent but sighed when he looked at me expectantly and patiently, the grin never fell from his face.

"I-I'm 25. Not a kid," my voice came out a bit muttered, but he just smiled wider.

"Older than my oldest but not by much. He's graduating this year and has been working his ass off to get into some fancy university for criminal justice. It's in New York, and I'm not looking forward to seeing my kid off."

"I-is that right?" I mutter, glancing at him. He just grins bigger and nods.

"Once you have kids, you'll understand. Luckily for me, I have a few more years with my youngest. He's 14 and smart as all hell. He ain't into sports like his brother, but he is good at art; always drawing on everything he can. Can't tell you how many times I caught him drawing on the walls," he says before laughing loudly. I had to force the smile from my lips, and we

ended up having a pretty good conversation though he mostly talked about his sons.

Next thing I know, I'm running through the woods with the man by my side. He had pulled me along whenever I started to fall behind, both of us breathing heavily though I suffered more. Something rammed into us, and I slid down a pretty steep hill. The impact had knocked the breath out of me, and I struggled to get it back. I gasped loudly for a few minutes before something landed by my hand.

It was a severed head with bloodied honey-blonde hair and empty gray eyes.

Tears streamed down my face, and I quickly turned to the side and vomited. I struggled to my feet, tripped over them a couple of times, and continued to run, ignoring the bloodcurdling screams behind me.

When I had to stop, I leaned against a gnarled pine tree and tried to catch my breath. I heard footsteps and scooted around the tree. An area felt caved in against my back, and it caught my attention. I looked behind me and saw a hole.

Something compelled me to look inside, but when I leaned over, a scream sounded only a few feet away from me.

****

I slowly sit up and some kind of weight falls from my waist. The image is the only thing floating in my head, and the next thing that I know, I'm sitting on the floor, leaning heavily over the coffee table. My hand moves quickly over this sheet of paper that I don't know where or when I got, a pen in hand as I scratch over the entire page.

A second after blinking, I see the rough sketch of a narrow, masculine face with neat dark hair that's combed over perfectly, and his features are average though they border handsome. The only thing that screams uncanny is the wide, painful smile.

I blink the haze from my mind, but I still feel a bit fuzzy. On top of the page, I scratch the words "Have You Been Having Strange Dreams?" and on the bottom, I write "Have You Seen This Man?"

"Chance!"

I jump and look behind me, seeing Isolde standing there; only wearing one of my shirts and her hair loose and messy. Worry clouds her eyes, and she gives me a small smile.

"I've been calling your name for the past five minutes. What's got you thinking so deeply?" She sits behind me, wraps her arms around my back, and nuzzles into my neck. She smells like my sandalwood body wash, but I catch a whiff of the green apple shampoo and blackberry body lotion she keeps leaving in my bathroom. The combination knocks my concentration for a second but ignore her question.

She leans further over my shoulder and hums softly.

"Whatcha drawing? Looks kinda creepy."

I can't believe that I'm just realizing that I only see him around the woods. Either that or he always chases me into them. Why is that? Is there something there? Does he get some kind of home-field advantage? Does he want me to get lost in there? Does he just enjoy chasing me like the sadist he is?

"Have you seen this man? Is this the guy you've been having nightmares about? If so, this might be a good coping habit for dealing with the mental scarring."

What about the howling? That's been happening more often and only occurs around the Man. What does it mean? Are they signaling that the Man is nearby? Are they warning me? Helping the Man? The claw marks on my windowsill were obviously from it, so that leaves the question of why. Why was he by my house? To send me a warning? To place a mark on my back? Was I chosen at random or was it always going to be me?

"Hey, did you hear that screaming last night? I swear, it sounded like it was right outside the window or something. Do you think it was a coyote?"

I walk over to my little office area and start making copies of the drawing, ignoring the background noise around me. I make a good stack, brush off the hand that tries to grab my shoulder, and walk out of the house, barely remembering to put on some shoes.

I have a job to do and no time for Isolde.

****

There's something almost therapeutic about the routine that I settle in. It's simple: place one of the copies on any suitable surface, staple it, and move on to the next one. It allows a blissful fog to settle over me. In the back of my mind, I notice how people come and go, cars drive by, and different people stare and talk, but, for once, it doesn't bother me. I'm finally able to enjoy the environment around me.

"Hey! If you keep ignoring me, I will have your ass in the cooler so fast your head would spin!" A low voice says.

When did he get here?

I glance back and see two cops standing not too far from me. After making that discovery, I bring my attention back to the matter at hand. I feel a tinge of unease as I realize that a lot of time has passed and I'm still not sure how long they've been here.

"Do you not understand English? I gotta say it in Spanish or something? Answer me when I'm talking to you," the same guy says.

"Look, man, I'm just hanging up fliers. I'm not doing anything wrong," I tell them. My voice sounds slurred in my ears, and I shake my head to try and clear my head.

"Right, just hangin' fliers," one of them says.

I finally look at them and take in the appearance of both cops. The younger one, the one who spoke, has dark brown hair in a buzzcut, dark brown eyes, and a mocking grin on his face. He looks like the type of jackass you would find in the bar, bragging about his high school days. The older one looks a bit more familiar, and I scan his features to try and see if it would come to me. He has dirty blonde hair styled in an undercut and is brushed back with plenty of gray streaked throughout, weary light gray eyes, and a scar that runs through his left eyebrow.

He must've seen me staring at it because he offered me a half-hearted smile.

"Yeah. That ain't illegal now, is it?"

"What is illegal is loitering and being a public disturbance, so I would drop the attitude, pal. You just *hangin' up fliers* is freaking out all of these good people."

"Then they can just leave. I'm not holding anyone hostage, I'm not talking to anybody, and, hell, I'm not even breathing in anyone's direction. Kids put fliers up for their dogs all the time, and no one gives them shit," I say, venom soaking in my words. Irritation swells inside when the young dick takes a step to me before his partner holds him back.

"Kids looking for their missing dog is a bit different than suspected murderers putting up creepy ass pictures."

"Hey! Nick, go wait in the squad car; I'll handle this," the older guy finally steps in.

"I'm not leaving you with this-"

"It wasn't a request."

The Nick guy shuts his mouth, gives me a harsh look, and walks to their car. Instead of getting in as the older guy ordered, he leans against it with his arms crossed and looks right in our direction. The older guy turns his attention back to me and nods to the fliers in my hand.

"Quite the drawing you got there. There a story behind it?"

"Look, I appreciate the concern, but I'm just minding my business. What do you want with me? Why can't you people just leave me alone?" He shifts on his feet and runs a hand over his head, a deep sigh leaving his mouth.

"Because I'm worried about you, Chance."

"The hell you mean?" Now I know there's something up with him. Just who is he? Another relative of one of the victims? Some vigilante trying to lower my guard? A random "civilian" trying to get the inside story?

"I knew your father. Jakob was a good man, and before he passed, I promised him I would've looked after you and Hawthorne, and I admit I haven't been doing too good of a job with that."

Now I remember him. I remember late nights staying up with my brother and father to watch ice hockey games, and Sam would come over with peach rings and cherry Coca-Cola, our favorite snacks. I remember gorging ourselves on them until we threw up, our dad and Sam cheering us on before our mother would yell at them. I remember Sam keeping my brother and me at his house when my father kept drinking himself into a stupor after my mother killed herself. I remember him throughout a lot of important events before the man seemingly disappeared when I was ten, around the time my dad died.

I also remember I never saw him at Hawthorne's funeral.

"So, you're sheriff now huh, Sam? Time does fly, but I guess that's to be expected when we haven't seen each other in, what, nine years?" I drawl, turning my body completely towards him.

"I deserved that."

"What's going on then? Are you looking to do some charity or is this some ploy to alleviate your guilt for bailing on me and Hawthorne? Has to be one of those things because I can't see any other reason for approaching me now."

Sam takes a step closer to me and places a hand on my shoulder, bringing a grimace to my face. Despite literally leaving my brother and me high and dry, I admit that there's still some warmth that comes from his friendly touch that I can't resist leaning into.

"If I gotta choose one, then it's the latter. I'm not gonna lie, I do feel guilty as hell for not being there for you two. It's too late to do anything for Hawthorne, I know that and I gotta take that to my grave, so I want to make it up to your old man and your brother by looking out for you," he says. His eyes seem to age a couple of years, and I feel like I have no choice but to swallow any bitterness. "Please, kiddo, let me have this. I don't need them handing my ass to me when I see them in the Afterlife."

The next few hours are spent hanging up the rest of the fliers, and Sam making conversation. I didn't want to talk at first, but his constant talking made it hard to fall back in my thoughts. He soon manages to pull more and more words out of me, and I find myself opening up to him. Hell, it's more like I finally find someone who listens, and when they don't dismiss me outright, I trauma dump.

I tell him about Isolde and my messed-up relationship with her. I tell him about the constant gossip going around. I tell him about the assault and have to talk him out of retaliating against Austin which felt pretty damn great. I tell him everything about what's going on, but I don't touch the Grinning Man. That's just the one topic I don't want to touch with him.

We finally put up the last one, and he turns to me with a smile.

"Thanks for the help, Sam. I kinda missed this," I admit.

"Me, too, kid. If you need anything, and I mean anything at all, you come and find me, alright? I swear I'm gonna be around more often, I just need you to reach out. My number and address are still the same."

With that, he strolls away with his phone in his hand. It feels good to reconnect with him, but I can't shake my hesitance in letting him in completely. I wasn't lying, I did miss him. I miss the feeling of someone genuinely looking out for me. I just don't see any good coming out of telling him that when the likely outcome is him thinking of me like everyone else; that I'm crazy.

Now that I'm done, I decide it's time to head back. Hopefully, Isolde is gone by now, I don't feel like having to explain why I left. I'm willing to bet that she'll make a bigger deal out of it than it is and will want to set up some impromptu session/interrogation.

As I am about to leave, though, I start to get that feeling that eyes were on me. You know, that burning, uncomfortable feeling on the back of your neck that travels down your spine, sending chills throughout your body. Like prey sensing the presence of the predator. Looking over my shoulder but not seeing anything, I start to move faster.

The whole way back, I can't shake the feeling of eyes on me.

Chapter 6

A few days go by, and I find myself talking with Izzy in my living room, my face in my hands. There's a cup of dark roast coffee in front of me and a cup of pomegranate juice in front of her. I rub my face and look at her as she writes something in a small pink notebook.

Today, she's wearing a pair of black suit pants and a long-sleeved formal shirt that seems to be made out of some flimsy material because I can see that she's wearing a blue bra, and her hair is done in that no-nonsense tight bun I usually see it in. I look down at my red and black plaid pajama pants, and some old System of a Down t-shirt that I found stuffed behind my dresser, and I don't even want to think about what my hair looks like. I grimace at the contrast before Izzy finally looks up at me as she puts down the notebook.

"So the dreams are getting worse?"

"A lot worse. I'm not just remembering the Man anymore. I just started remembering the group and how they died," I mutter. I take a deep breath as I remember the blonde man who loved to talk about his sons. "It's brutal. It's always brutal."

Izzy perks up and smiles, her eyes twinkling.

"Are you serious? Chance, that's great!"

What the actual fuck is wrong with her?

"Great?" I cut my eyes to her, and her mouth slowly turns down. "Yeah, *great*. It's so great having to relive watching everyone around you die, one by one. It's great having to see them decapitated, dismembered, and disemboweled. It's great having to constantly look over your shoulder because the whole town thinks you're a psychotic murderer. It's great wondering which form of abuse is gonna hit me next: physical or verbal?"

"Chance, a couple of bad experiences don't prove that the world is out to get you."

"But it proves how far the ones who are will go. I have a target on my back, Isolde, and the very few people who care won't care enough to do anything. It's like they're waiting for me to get hurt before they actually talk."

"That's not fair, and you know it. We are trying to help, but you keep pushing us away. You push *me* away."

We're just talking in circles. Again. The story of our lives.

I roll my eyes and figure it's best to stop entertaining her. It must've been written on my face because, in the next second, she was sitting next to me and holding my arm. Her touch is comforting yet I cringe away from it. Her face drops before a gleam forms in her eye. Izzy digs through her purse and hands me a piece of paper.

"I've been meaning to give you this and now seems like the perfect time. This is going to help you."

"What is it?"

"A prescription for Versacloz. Some of the more common side effects include blurred vision, confusion, fever, shakiness in the legs, arms, hands, or feet, drowsiness, or fainting just to name a few," she explains. "I know that it seems like a whole lot of cons, but this is more effective than your current prescription."

I look down at the small slip of paper in my hand, doubt swelling inside. It seems pretty risky, but what other choice do I have? Maybe with this I can finally get a good night's sleep. I mutter out my thanks and a bright smile lights up her face as if I hung up the stars for her. We spend the next two hours just talking, and I can feel myself just relaxing in my seat; soaking up the normality. Her blue eyes look at me thoughtfully, and a small smile forms on her lips.

"Chance, what are we?" That stuns me for a minute.

"What?"

"I mean, we just argue, have sex, and argue some more. The few times that we do get along always end with you pushing me away," she says, sighing deeply. "We've been together for four years and nothing in whatever this is has changed."

"I just have a lot going on right now, Isolde. In case you didn't notice, I'm going through some shit. A relationship is the last thing on my mind."

"And how long are you going to use that as an excuse? How long do I have to wait until you're ready?" I laugh a little and stare at her, trying to see if she's serious.

Judging by her expression, I'm gonna say very.

"Do you remember when we first met?" I ask, leaning back on the couch. Her eyes widen a bit, and her lips purse.

"Of course."

"I was so numb that day. Hawthorne was my best friend, my confidant, my everything, and when he died, it was like he took a piece of me with him. Ever since, I would always catch myself looking slightly towards the left whenever I would crack a joke, expecting to hear his laugh again," I tell her. My lips pull up into a smile as I think about his auburn hair that he could never tame or that crooked nose from getting into one too many fights. "I always set myself up for disappointment and hurt."

"I think the whole town remembers. His death affected all of us."

"Then someone suggested you to me, and after just two appointments we're fucking on your desk. Crazy how things work out, huh?"

"Why are you bringing this up now?" Her eyes glisten as she glares at me.

"Just tired of you trying to take the moral high ground."

I watch as she huffs and struggles to decide what to do with her hand as a hurt expression flickers across her face. I don't know what I feel watching her indecision, whether it's annoyance or regret, so I decide to take the initiative to pull her closer. A vulnerable smile appears, and, for once, I feel like maybe this was the right move. She straddles my lap and her arms loop around my neck. Her breasts press against my chest just right, before she presses her plump lips against mine, quickly bringing me into a familiar rhythm. Her hips grind down on mine, and I feel an immediate reaction, my body shuddering and my stomach tightening.

I watch her as she moves over me, and I gulp softly. Should I be doing this? However, when I feel her warm hand sneak inside my pants and gently grip me, I decide to lose myself in her embrace.

Just one more time.

****

Some hours later, I find myself staring blankly at the ceiling. The mind-numbing high still runs through my veins, and I realize how much I would kill for a cigarette. The cool air hits my feverish chest just right, and the long, slender arm lying over my stomach wraps around me tightly.

"I love you," she breathes against my skin.

My heart drops, and my mouth goes dry, making it painful to swallow. Needless to say, I don't give her the response she wants. This leads to dressing in silence, clenched jaws, and an air of uncertainty. I feel bad admitting this, but I can finally breathe when I hear the car peel out though a heavy weight settles in my chest. Why did she have to go and say that? Why would she go and ruin the balance we have? Why complicate it with a bullshit confession? Like we don't know what this really is?

I shuffle through a kitchen drawer, pushing aside empty bottles before I finally find some. I drop the two pills on the counter, grab a half-empty bottle of Jack Daniels, and down them both. With that done, I throw myself on the couch and put an arm over my eyes. A deep groan leaves me when someone starts banging on my door, and just when I decide to ignore it, the continuous knocks get louder.

Why the hell can't I get a break? When I throw it open, I see a red-faced, distraught Sibyl holding one of my fliers in her hands.

"Chance, what the fuck is going on?"

****

The two of us are sitting in front of us, our mugs have gone cold as I stare at her, but she stares at the mug in her hands. She's no longer crying, but her eyes are swollen and red. Her hands tremble, sloshing the liquid inside.

"Sibyl, I need you to get into exact details; it's important. Don't leave out anything."

"Okay, first, I just wanna say that I didn't even know I was dreaming; it was crazy! I seriously thought I was outside. I mean, I was even my favorite sportswear; these navy-blue PINK leggings, a gray sports bra, and these really comfy Lululemon shoes. The whole outfit was cute-"

She hiccups and starts to blink rapidly. I can't stop my leg from bouncing, and I resist the urge to snap at her as she takes a minute to wipe her face.

"But I've recently started feeling like blue isn't my color, so-"

"*Focus*!" I force myself to settle down when she flinches. "S-sorry, I- you- j-just, please focus."

She nods softly and blows her nose loudly on the napkin I gave her.

"Like I said, I was outside walking down the sidewalk, just minding my business. It was, like, really quiet, and I just started feeling creeped out. I'm talking massive heeby jeebies. I thought I was just being paranoid because I had watched a horror movie earlier, but something was just really bugging me.

I wanted to turn back and go home, I *know* I wanted to go home, but I just kept moving forward. Then, I started hearing this wolf howling close to me but I still didn't turn back or even start running. I just kept walking. That's when I saw it come from the woods. This thing was *huge*. I'm talking massive! It was completely black and had red eyes, and I thought it would immediately attack me but nope; it just stood there. I was so focused on him, that I almost missed the person walking in front of me."

"The Grinning Man," I mutter. She softly scoffs and leans back in her chair.

"Stupid name but yeah. That guy. He was dancing in front of me all weird and shit, and his head was in a really weird angle. We ended up making eye contact, and, after that, he started running backward, still looking at me. It was so freaky!"

"What happened next?"

"What do you think? I ran like hell! I went into the woods and just kept running. But then... I heard someone screaming. It sounded like a dude, and he was calling out for help," she says. She's quiet for a minute before huffing under her breath. "But I just kept running. I never looked back."

I recognize that look on her face and place my hand over hers. A small smile twitches on her lips, and she gives me a short nod.

"And then?"

"Then, the Grinning Man was in front of me. I screamed and finally woke up. My pillow was drenched, my eyes stung, and my chest hurt so fucking much. I thought it was just a really bad dream until I went downstairs and saw my front door slightly open," she says. "And if that wasn't enough, I saw claw marks scratched deep into the wood."

A heavy silence falls over us as we just stare at each other when a few hard knocks break through the atmosphere, and we both jump. Sibyl's eyes widen as she nervously moves to her feet, and my body moves despite my wishes, putting myself between the door and her. Her hands grip my arm tightly, and we stand motionless, staring at the door.

Dread fills my body and adrenaline rushes through my veins as I map out all possible escape routes. Is it The Grinning

Man? If we have to get away, it'll be a challenge; he moves pretty quickly, but he also sways like a drunkard which will slow him down some. I also notice that he has to make direct eye contact before chasing after you, so we can use that to our advantage. Or maybe it's that Austin guy, again; not satisfied with beating and deciding to just finish the job. What about any of the other residents of Grimsby? Hell, even that officer from the other day is suspicious. Fuck, too many factors, too many enemies.

I feel a hard nudge against my back, and I look over my shoulder to see Sibyl gesture impatiently towards the door. A minute of silent argument ends with me losing.

So, I walk carefully to the door, grab the knob, and slowly pull it open, peeking through the small opening. Instead of seeing a tall mass murderer, a violent asshole looking for revenge, or even some gothic punk wanting to vandalize more of my stuff, I see two well-dressed men waiting with solemn expressions. The taller one with dark hair peppered with gray immediately brings attention to himself.

"Are you Chance Curran?"

"Y-yes? I-is something wrong?"

The two men look at each other before the dark-haired one steps forward and shows some kind of identification.

"Mr. Curran, you are coming with us. You're under arrest for murder."

Chapter 7

I wish I could say that I'm surprised to be sitting in an interrogation room, but I'm more surprised that it took this long.

The air is cold, there's an oppressive quiet hanging over us, and the hard wooden chair under my ass has me constantly shifting in place. It doesn't help that a heavy gaze settles on my head after an hour of ignoring me. I look at the empty, bland walls as I think back to how I got here; the humiliation that I felt as I was stuffed in the back of their car, and the stares in my direction as the car rode slowly through town.

I can't wait to hear the new stories they're going to come up with.

"So, Chance, let's try to get some things straight, okay? My name is Detective Brooks, and I'm with the homicide unit. Since this is our first time meeting, why don't we lay some groundwork? Let's start with your name and age," he says.

The man is African-American with a stocky build, black hair styled in a military-esque crop, and dark brown eyes that seem to glare right through me. He's dressed like you would expect from a detective on TV with his white dress shirt, black dress pants, black suspenders, and a clear gun holster on his left side.

I catch my eyes drifting down to it a couple of times, and when my eyes meet his, his eyes seem to become colder as if daring me to do something.

"Chance Curran, and I'm 26," I say, running my free hand over my face. The handcuff on my other wrist clinks, and I lightly tug at it under his watchful eyes.

"Birthday? Family?"

"November 1st," I pause and tug at the cuffs again. "No family."

"Any girlfriend? Boyfriend?"

"It's… complicated."

"What's complicated?"

"A very confusing Facebook status; how the fuck am I supposed to respond to that? Complicated is complicated."

His jaw tightens, and his fists clench before relaxing and leaning back in his seat. Brooks picks up a folder that I'm just noticing and sets it in the middle of the table, pushing it toward me with his index finger.

"Alright, smartass, since you want to play cute, let's get down to business. Open the folder," he commands, his voice clear and steady despite the anger lying underneath, threatening to break the surface.

Slowly under his watchful gaze, I open it and can feel my brows furrow when I register that I'm looking at various pictures. I look at him in confusion, but he just gestures at them. I pick up the small stack and a choked sob struggles to leave my throat. My heart plummets to my stomach, and my breathing starts to pick up to the point that I might start hyperventilating.

The first picture shows a male with deep gashes on his body, the most prominent one being the one across his neck almost decapitating him. He's lying in some ditch where obvious bite marks are on his body, mostly on his arms and legs.

"Jesus Martinez; 35, veterinarian, engaged and set to be married in the Summer, and no kids but had three dogs everyone said he loved more than anything. Those bite marks?

Antemortem. Poor bastard was, miraculously and unfortunately, still alive when the animals started eating him," Brooks informs me. I let the picture fall from my hand and focus on the next one.

The second one shows a young woman with a broken neck set at a disturbing angle, an angle that's similar to the Grinning Man's, but it isn't the only thing broken. Both arms are bent at an acute angle, the bone straining so much that it almost breaks through the skin, and her legs bent that same way at the knees, almost causing her toes to touch her chest.

"Destiny Wilson; 29, primary caregiver for her mother with Alzheimer's, married with a beautiful baby girl that loves animals. Destiny wanted to take pictures of some wild animals to show her daughter. The last words she told her husband were to make sure he didn't tell their daughter what she was doing because she wanted it to be a surprise."

I don't want to see any more.

The third one shows a heavyset man with his intestines spilling out from the large gash cut neatly across his lower stomach that almost looks surgical. His arms lay limply around it as if he was trying in vain to keep them from spilling.

"Owen Taylor; 40, not married with any kids, owned a traveling food stall that specialized in deep-dish pizzas, Philly cheese steak subs, and loaded fries, and was a frequent visitor of his local bar, always there for every football game. Patrons described him as boisterous but generous. One of his employees brought him the ticket for the tour as a thank-you for hiring him when he was down on his luck. In case you couldn't tell from the blood trail underneath him and his broken bleeding nails, he tried desperately to crawl to safety. Didn't get very far."

The fourth photo shows a limbless and headless naked torso impaled by a sharp branch, keeping it suspended in the air. Arms could be seen on the ground under it, propped upright with the hands clasped together and holding a cross necklace. I don't see the legs anywhere… nor the head.

"Miranda White; 32, a recovering heroin addict, two years sober, an occasional motivational speaker who warned about the dangers of drugs, and an aspiring artist who managed to commission some of her paintings. Her work is a bit dark, but a lot of critics remark that they all have some sort of hopeful element hidden in the work. I didn't see any of that, but I don't have much of an artistic eye so I'll take their word for it. Whoever did that to her has their artistic flair."

The fifth one shows a feminine figure that appears more like one giant bruise than an actual person. Unlike the others, she doesn't have any slashes or bites. Based on the bumps, bruises, and broken jaw, it's clear she was beaten to death.

"Ferrah Clark; 23, hairdresser, cosmetologist, and newly divorced. Managed to finally get away from her abusive ex and volunteered at a women's shelter to give free makeovers to them; claimed that every woman deserved to feel beautiful. Wasn't looking too pretty in the end, huh?"

I'm exhausted but still look at the sixth picture and see a man cut in half Black Dahlia style. His upper body shows he was on his stomach, and his arms were covering the back of his head. All I can hear is a young man, trying hard to be an adult yet brought to the peak of desperation, crying for his mother.

"Johnathan Dean; 24, single, an only child, and a mechanic. Fancied himself a real James Dean, and his mother said that when she brought him a black leather jacket for his 18th birthday, he never took it off; even started to keep a cigarette in his mouth. Just for show, though, he had weak lungs but wanted the whole look; I mean, the kid got the Spyder and everything. Unfortunately, those weren't the only things he shared with Dean."

I recognize the seventh one as I stare at the familiar honey-blonde curls that are saturated in blood and empty gray eyes staring past the camera. The head is separate and is the only thing visible in the frame.

"Jacob Haze; 35, single father of two, worked construction all around town and was a volunteer firefighter. Loved exploring the wilderness and especially loved doing it with his kids. Lots of people around town said he was excited to see his son graduate, bragging to everyone who would listen that his boy was going to graduate with honors. Now, the only thing his kids could bury was his head. God knows where the body is."

The eighth one shows two bodies clinging tightly to each other, the smaller body, probably female, has its head leaning against the other's, probably male, chest. Their bodies are pinned together through a sharp branch that's impaling the woman's head and the man's chest. The bodies seem like they're hiding in some bushes. Lot of good that did.

"Michael and Jennifer Young; 53 and 52 respectively, married for 30 years, both retired, him from the postal office and her from 911 dispatch, five kids, seven grandkids, and three dogs. Being able to finally enjoy their golden years, they decided to see the world, Alaska was the current step and Hawaii was the next. Told the grandkids they were gonna take pictures and send postcards. The oldest of their kids thought a closed-casket funeral would be best for obvious reasons."

The star of the tenth picture is a lean man propped against a tree, legs spread in front of him, arms resting on his lap, and his chin resting on his chest. There are no wounds on him, nothing to hint at how he died. If it wasn't for the empty eyes looking forward, I would think he just fell asleep or something.

"Thomas Nguyen; 30, newly married with no kids, chemistry teacher at a private school, and enjoys playing guitar at his local café to a pretty good turnout. His wife was supposed to come on the tour, too, but she got a pretty high fever the day before. Convinced him to go without her, and that his mother would watch over her; didn't want to waste the ticket. We had no clue what killed him, and we ultimately had to put it down to heart failure. Our Forensic Pathologists had no idea what happened. The only thing they said was that, despite no prior history of medical problems, his heart just gave out."

The 11th picture is the weirdest one so far, and for a minute, I don't even know what I'm looking at. I bring it closer to my face and immediately have to put it back down when I register what I'm seeing, I throw it on the table. At first glance, all you can see is a pine tree with a small hole in it, but when you look closer, you can see a body broken and stuffed inside, pushed as far in as possible.

"Felix Colden; 20, single, orphaned, and a college dropout. He was down in the morgue a lot longer than the others since no one came to identify him until his former dorm roommate was finally contacted. The guy was distraught. He gave Felix the ticket for the tour since Felix managed to get a job interview at his dream job working at some big comic store. It's not uncommon for celebrities to appear there to sign the comics of the characters they play. Things were looking up, and he was a week away from the interview when he went on this tour."

The final one shows a barely recognizable person, but I remember those golden locks of big curls that belonged to the kid of the group. Her picture is the worst one… her body is dangling from a tree branch, but I can't tell what her noose is. Her neck is broken, and I can only pray that this happened before the rest of her injuries. The reason? She's missing her shirt completely, but nothing explicit is showing because the skin of her torso is stripped clean off, showing the bloody muscles underneath. Chunks of meat are taken from her body, and it's startling the contrast between the gruesome view of her torso and her intact head and lower body.

"And that's Amanda Lee; 15, a high school student with decent grades, recently started dating someone in her math class, libero on the volleyball team, and the youngest of five. Family and friends said she was popular and made friends with everybody. No one had a bad thing to say about her. A week after her burial, one of her brothers found their mother hanging in Amanda's bedroom."

"I didn't do this. I-I-I couldn't do this," I tell him, my voice so quiet I could barely hear it. I put the pictures back on the table and shove them away from myself, but Brooks quickly moves them back, spreading them out so I can see each one.

"You couldn't do this *alone*. So, this Dancing Man. Was he your accomplice? Trying to pin all of the murders on him?"

"N-no, t-that's n-not-"

"Guess there's no honor amongst thieves, right?"

"H-h-he did it h-himself-!"

"Admit it!"

"I-I-I didn't-"

"ADMIT IT!"

He slams his fist on the table, and I flinch back, curling in on myself and trying to block out his voice. As I try to ignore him, I notice a burning, stinging sensation on my arms. When I look at them I realize that I've been picking at them at some point and they are dripping thin trails of blood.

I don't want to be here; I want to go home. Why won't he leave me alone? Why doesn't he believe me? Why doesn't anybody believe me?

I don't know why, but I slam my head on the table and bury my face in my arms. The anger radiating from Brooks is suffocating, and my heart starts to pound even harder as I can feel him getting closer when the door opens.

"Brooks, I can take it from here," a new voice says.

"Good luck. Keep me updated."

"Of course, man. Take it easy."

It's quiet for a few minutes, and I take the time to try and stabilize myself.

"Look, I'm sorry about my partner; things have been pretty hectic, as you can imagine. My name is Detective Cailan Lachlan. Can I get you anything? Water? A cigarette? Something warm?" the new guy, Lachlan, asks with a smile.

He has sandy blonde hair, stumbles on his square jaw, and hazel brown eyes that contradict his smile. I scoff and look at him through my arms, my eyes feeling raw after the interaction with Brooks.

"I thought the whole good-cop-bad-cop gimmick was only something you see in movies."

"What can we say? We love a classic," he laughs, but I remain silent. He nods his head in acceptance before messing with the files in hand, and I watch him, wondering if he's going to show me pictures, too. Instead, he quietly looks at me.

Then, he starts to hand me a picture, and I'm already preparing for the worst as I sit up. The pictures show a dead woman sitting against a tree and hope swells up when I notice the numerous bite marks on her. She died from an animal attack. I hear him clear his throat, and I realize that I've been smiling. I quickly wipe it from my face.

"So, why are you showing me this? Looks like a wolf or something got to her," I ask him. He takes it back and nods his head.

"You'd be correct, however… we found human hair and thorns from a blackberry bush on the body, and it was located about half a mile from your house. Can you see why you were brought in?"

"When did you find the body?"

"Sunday, but we suspect she was killed Thursday."

The night Isolde heard that scream.

Isolde…

"I have an alibi! I-I was with Isolde, Dr. Isolde Ashford that night."

"Would she verify that claim?"

"Of course!"

He nods, tells me he'll be back soon, and leaves the room. I'm finally able to catch my breath, running my hand over my face.

This is good. This is great! I'm finally one step closer to clearing my name and maybe even getting the authority to recognize the Grinning Man as an actual threat. They already acknowledge that I couldn't have done this by myself; now they have to acknowledge I didn't do this at all. They fucking finally have to investigate whoever or whatever the Grinning Man is.

Lachlan comes back after some time, and I lean my body toward him after he sits back down.

"Don't keep me in suspense; am I free to go?"

"No," he says clearly and casually. I swallow back whatever I'm about to say, and my mouth opens and closes.

"What? Why not? I was with Isolde that night and *all* night. I couldn't have killed anybody."

"The problem, Chance, is that Dr. Ashford didn't corroborate with your story. So, I'll ask again," Lachlan levels a heavy stare on me, "where were you the night of the murder?"

I have to blink a couple of times when my eyes start to burn, and I struggle to swallow as the walls start to close in on me from all sides.

"Can I have that cigarette now?"

Time passes by, and I'm smoking my third cigarette as Lachlan continues the interrogation, his voice never raising to Brooks' level but firm nonetheless. Even as he's asking questions, the only thing going through my mind is: why the fuck Isolde would do this?

Even if our relationship is messed up, that doesn't mean she should've lied about this. Lied about something that could land me either life or death row. She saw what the fucking people in town would do; what does she think the law is going to do?

Someone else knocks on the door, and I drag my eyes to it, finding out it's some random guy instead of Brooks like I was expecting. Lachlan walks with him out of the room, but the door is cracked open.

Even though they're talking quietly to themselves, I'm able to strain my ears enough and focus on what they're saying. The first person I hear is the other detective.

"Sir, bad news. The test came back."

"And?"

"Not a match. It wasn't him."

It's painfully quiet for a minute before I hear something hit the wall hard.

"Dammit!"

"What do we do now, sir?"

"What else can we do? We let him go,"

"But-"

The door opens again, and I move my eyes back forward, straightening up in my chair.

"You're free to go, but my suggestion?" Detective Lachlan levels a hard stare at me, and I numbly meet his gaze. "Don't leave town."

****

I find myself standing outside of Whole Latte Love, and the sight feels like discovering a bottle of water after being stranded in the middle of the ocean.

My brother and I used to love coming here all the time. We would do chores all week just to save up money and get their famous Boston cream pie and a cup of hot chocolate, specially made with a heap of whipped cream, chocolate syrup drizzled on top, massive marshmallows, chocolate sprinkles, and a peppermint candy cane.

Walking inside, I'm hit with a burst of warm air, the scent of freshly ground coffee, the warm glow of the soft lighting, and a wave of nostalgia completes the

"Welcome- oh!" the feminine speaker perks up and smiles happily as we make eye contact. Soon, a petite elderly woman hustles as fast as she can from around the counter before wrapping her arms around me tightly. It takes a minute before I return it, and I bend down (way down – she's about five feet even) to her height. The scent of paint, honeysuckles, and, strangely enough, the aftermath of heavy rain. It's a weird combination that washes over me, but I soak it in regardless.

"It's good to see you, Miss Darcy," I mutter.

"Well, well, well; look who decided to show his face," a familiar, jovial voice muses, French accent strong. The grin on my face widens when I look and see Arthur approaching us. He quickly joins in on our little impromptu group hug.

Darcy and Arthur Moore; an 84-year-old couple who have been married for over 60 years and in love for even longer. They're the owners of the café and knew my family long before my parents even got together. Arthur Moore is a French immigrant who came here for business as he worked as a traveling photographer. Whenever someone asks how he met

Darcy, an Alaskan native, he goes into great detail about their meeting, always ending the story by "coming for the beautiful views but staying for his beautiful, future wife."

They're the picture of a perfect, healthy relationship.

"You finally decide to come here, mon papillon?"

"I know, I know… it's just been hectic lately," I say. I move away from them and sit at my usual booth, a table against the wall but has a window right by it, making for the best spot to look out at the world without fear of it looking back.

Darcy is already making a hot chocolate while Arthur prepares a plate for me.

"Oh, trust me, we know. Which is why we were expecting you to come," he says. "So why didn't you?"

"I didn't want to drag you two into this mess. They're already bold enough to attack me on the streets, I don't doubt that they'll do something to you two or, at least, the shop."

"Stop worrying about us, we can handle ourselves," Darcy scolds. She hands me the mug of hot chocolate and glares down at me. "You know whenever anything bad happens, you come here to us. No matter what it is."

"Couldn't have said it better myself," Arthur chimes in, placing a plate in front of me. On it is a chocolate drizzled croissant with fruits on top and a slice of Boston cream pie; both fresh and both having a mouthwatering scent.

The second they turn around and head back behind the counter, I whip out my flask and pour in Jack Daniel's. I stuff it back in the pocket and stir it with the candy cane.

"Hey, is this seat taken?" a mature voice asks, startling me.

Looking up, I see this otherworldly young woman with thick, straight, raven black hair falling to her waist, dark blue eyes framed by long eyelashes, and skin so pale that I can see the blue veins teasing the surface. She's wearing a tight, long-sleeved black dress which was rather revealing and low cut, black, almost sheer stockings, black wedged boots, and many gothic bracelets and necklaces decorating her person, the most prominent one being a familiar black cross necklace.

I only realize that I've been watching her a little too intensely when her blood-red painted lips pull into a teasing smile. My cheeks heat up, and I look down at my mug, distracting myself by taking another gulp.

"Saint Michael's."

"What?"

"The cross. You've been looking at it closely, I thought you might have been curious," she explains. She gestures to the booth, and I snap out of it, smiling at her. She gracefully slides into the seat in front of me.

"I-I wasn't- I-I mean-"

"It's fine," she reassures. Her eyes scan over my face, and she clasps her hands under her chin. "Now, what has gotten you thinking so deeply?

There is something about the chick in front of me that keeps pulling my attention, and I feel my face heating up when I catch her soft, blue eyes.

"Y- you're gonna think I'm crazy," I breathed out. Her response is a smile that leaves me breathless and dazed.

"Try me."

"Well, the whole town thinks I murdered a bunch of people and that I'm psychotic because I believe that a Man was there and did it."

"A man? Why would that be strange? Shouldn't they investigate that?"

Fuck does it feel good to hear that.

"It's because of the way I described him. The Man has this creepy ass grin, dances instead of walking normally, and is always looking up at the sky."

"Sounds terrifying! Maybe a drunk? Or even someone with a mental illness?"

"That's what I was thinking, but I'm also considering him to be some kind of paranormal creature," I admit before drinking more of my hot chocolate.

"Why's that?"

"I've been having weird dreams about him. He's always chasing after me, but the dreams feel more like visions. So, I've been thinking that the Man is some sort of creature that can communicate telepathically."

The girl looks at me in wonder, and I can feel my cheeks heat up. I brace myself for the laughter or even the look of disgust along with the shout of "psycho," but I get neither.

"Well, that's certainly the predicament," she says, not a hint of judgment on her face.

"So, you believe me?" she looks at me apologetically, but I can't bring myself to resent her for it.

"Not exactly… I mean, it's quite the claim. It's like you're asking me to believe in vampires or werewolves."

"Why do I hear a 'but' in this sentence?"

"*But* I don't believe in impossibility. Who knows what's out there?"

We smile at each other, and I find myself getting more comfortable in my seat. Before I knew it, I just started to spill about everything.

I tell her about the fucked up "relationship" with Isolde and the shit she did to me at the police station, how the relationship started, and how I truly felt about the whole thing, and I laugh hard at her response.

"What a toxic bitch."

Then I start talking about the isolation, the inadequacy, the self-hatred, the uncertainty; just everything that's plaguing me proceeds to spill out as naturally and smoothly as water. The whole time, I notice how her eyes never stray from mine, and she always nods or makes some sort of verbal indication that she's listening.

Just like Isolde, but… this is different.

Her version of listening seems obligatory, but this woman seems genuinely interested in every word from my mouth.

This woman.

"I-I'm sorry, what did you say your name was?" I shake my head and laugh a little. "I-it probably helps to introduce myself first. My name is Chance. It's nice to meet you."

"It's nice to meet you, Mr. Curran," she laughs gently and steals a strawberry from my croissant, placing it in her mouth. "Though, I never met anyone with that name before. Did your parents have a reason for naming you that?"

"Yeah, after they had my older brother, they didn't want any more kids. Took almost all of the precautions to prevent it, yet here I am. Chance sounded better than Surprise, and that's that."

"Simple yet cute; a chance baby. Were you close with your family?"

"Oh yeah!" I answer almost immediately, perking up in my seat. "My mom, Aria, was a neurologist and even when she would come home dead tired, she would still make time for us, and my dad, Jakobi, was a stay-at-home dad. He always tried to make everything fun and keep us active."

"And your brother?"

My brother.

How could I even describe him in a way to do him justice?

"Hawthorne was… the best brother anyone could ask for. It didn't matter how busy he was or how he was feeling, he always put me first and made sure everything was all right with me. He was just so fucking selfless," I sigh heavily as the memories start to flow. "Not only that, but he also never once made me feel like I was the annoying baby brother. Always including me whenever he goes out to have fun with his friends and never letting them give me crap. He was my hero."

"He sounds like a great guy," she says.

"He was."

She smiles before squeezing my hand.

"I somewhat wish I had a sister. For some reason, I always imagined an older sister and me dancing at some fancy ball, trying to capture the most eligible bachelor's attention," she admits a sheepish smile on her lips. "Pretty silly, right?"

"Strangely, I can picture that, but with that all-black ensemble, you'd probably find yourself burned at the stake before dancing with your Mr. Darcy," I tell her, unable to keep myself from laughing at my little joke.

"Or hung, stoned, starved, drowned, et cetera. So many fun possibilities," she says, matching my energy.

We spend the next few hours just talking about this and that, Darcy or Arthur occasionally appearing with more things to snack on. A text comes through my phone and ignore it when I see the sender but notice how late it is.

"I'm guessing from that expression that it's time to go?"

"Unfortunately," I mutter, hands playing with a sugar packet. We sit for a few seconds before she starts to laugh quietly, and I bite my lip to try and keep my smile down.

My phone vibrates again, and she lightly touches my hand.

"Aren't you going to go?"

"Unfortunately," this time, I don't fight back the smile. She rolls her eyes as she smiles back at me and pulls me up.

"Come on, no more stalling. Besides, I should be going myself."

"Fine, if you wanna get rid of me that much," I throw her some sad eyes, but she puts a cold hand on my back and pushes me to the entrance. From the corner of my eye, I see Darcy and Arthur waving at us with matching grins on their faces.

"You're cute but not that cute."

"At least let me walk you home," I playfully plead with her as we slow down a bit at the door.

"Sorry, I don't take strangers home, but," she trails off, a smile teasing her lips. "Maybe after a few more dates?"

I smile and hold open the door for her.

"I'll hold you to that."

With that, she practically glides away, and I'm left watching her back as it gradually disappears. When I go to leave, it's only then that I realize I never got her name.

Thankfully this isn't the last time we're going to see each other.

Time to head back. I can't wait to see her again.

And with that thought in mind, I head back home with a bit more pep in my step.

Chapter 8

Well, this is just as expected.

The first thing that I notice is the weird substance (maybe shaving cream?) covering the walls, words spray painted on the side (as usual) that read "burn in Hell" as well as some other pleasant expletives, and the classic toilet paper thrown over the house and some of the trees.

The second thing I notice is the familiar blonde leaning against a black car, his arms crossed and his face void of any emotion.

Well, fuck.

I guess the silver lining to all of this is that Isolde isn't here. Glass half full and all that crap.

I walk towards Austin, hands in my pockets, and he meets me halfway, his hands clenched at his sides.

"Austin, I thought our last encounter meant you didn't exactly like being around me, so consider me very fucking confused to see you here."

"And consider me very fucking pissed that they let you out again. How many more people do you have to kill before they finally lock you up?"

I don't try to stop the groan from leaving my lips or my eyes from rolling, and he takes another step forward.

"And how many times do I have to be investigated and released until everyone realizes I'm innocent?"

"Innocent is a pretty strong wrong considering the shit that follows you."

"Oh, did your criminology degree teach you that?"

"Funny. I figured you would be sniveling and groveling by now. Isn't that your MO? Crying and trying to convince everyone you're innocent even with bodies behind you?"

I run my fingers through my hair and sigh heavily.

"What do you want?"

"What do I want?" Austin grabs my shirt tightly, pulling me closer. "I want these killings to stop. I want to sleep better at night knowing another piece of shit is off the streets. I *want* to not have to constantly look over my shoulder, wondering when the next murder will happen or who the next victim's gonna be, always worrying if it's gonna be my brother."

"And you don't think I want all of that?" I scream back at him, pushing him back. "You think I like living in fear, wondering who's gonna fuck me over next? When's the next time I'm gonna get federal attention for some crime I didn't commit?"

"Would you quit acting like the fucking victim? It's pathetic!"

"Acting like the victim? I am the victim! I'm a victim of a small-town mentality! I am a victim of some serial killer! Face it; you can act as tough as you want, but the fact of the matter is you would've crumbled if you faced half the shit I go through. Fuck, you might have already eaten lead by now."

The inevitable punch knocks me to the ground, and I brace myself as he straddles me, as for a second time, he starts aiming punches at my face. I ignore the hits contacting my face and try to do my damage the best I can from my position on my back.

We're exchanging hits, but my anger numbs me to them. The attacks only seem to fuel aggression and set me further on the offense.

"What's it going to take before you guys realize what the true threat is? I'm the only one trying to investigate this thing, and you're holding me back!" I spit out before grunting after a particularly hard hit to the jaw.

"Do you fucking hear yourself? And you wonder why everyone thinks you're a fucking psychopath! I bet you get off on that shit!"

"Fuck you, man!"

It seems like the fighting gets more intense to the point where we focus only on each other. The fight itself becomes a bit of a blur, but I know that, at one point, I head-butt him, busting my forehead open.

I vaguely hear the sound of gravel being disturbed before seeing a familiar ginger appear behind Austin, pulling at his arm.

"Freaking. Let. Go," she grunts with each word, but Austin just yanks his arm back and goes back to punching me. "Ugh! Seriously?"

Austin grunts loudly and shifts off of me to the side. I'm breathing heavily but look at him as his expression shifts to one of disbelief, and he's clutching his head. A quick look at Sibyl, and I can see her arm poised in the air with her purse in hand.

"Are you packing fucking bricks?" Austin asks incredulously.

"I only carry the essentials! Now, are you going to keep acting like a meat head or can you sit pretty and listen to what we have to say?"

"Are you seriously defending a killer?"

Sibyl rolls her eyes and helps me to my feet, pulling out some napkin that I find has a fragrant floral scent, and pressing it to my nose. I'm pretty sure it's broken or something given how difficult it is to breathe at the moment.

"Look, we have more important things to do than figure out who's prettier, okay? It's me. Now, let's go," she says.

"Go where exactly?"

"Duh! To find that smiling guy and stop him!"

"It's the Grinning Man. Not super important, but it's the nuance of it," I quip, pressing the napkin harder to my nose. Sibyl elbows me before walking towards Austin who takes a step back.

"What are you talking about? You believe the crap he's spewing?"

"Considering that I saw him myself, yeah, I do."

"You saw him?" Austin scoffs, his eyes narrowing at her. "Yeah, sure you did. Question: what are you snorting and did you at least get it cheap?"

"I know this sounds stupid which is why you're coming with us to find him!"

"Excuse the fuck outta me?"

✱✱✱✱✱✱✱✱✱✱✱✱

"This is so fucking ridiculous."

"Shut up," Sibyl says, waving a hand in Austin's direction. He raises a brow at her and she somehow returns it with more attitude than I thought possible given her down-bad behavior earlier.

Austin sighs deeply.

"Can you at least tell me again what we're looking for?"

"A silver pocket watch," I mutter.

"A silver pocket watch that we both saw the Grinning Man drop in our dreams. After we found out that we saw the same thing, we realized that he dropped it around this area," Sibyl continues.

"Then how the hell would we find it if you dreamed it?"

"Like we said, he's real, and we both saw the same thing. It has to be here," Sibyl stresses.

"And if it's not?"

"It's here."

We're currently crawling around on the grass in a park looking for this pocket watch, two of us praying to catch a flash of silver. We told Austin that this was the area where the Grinning Man was in our dreams and it took some time, but we finally managed to get Austin to follow us here. Now, we can only hope to find it soon and prove to him that we're telling the truth. I mean, how can you explain two people having the same dream of the same person dropping the same thing?

Some time passes, and I notice Austin increasingly becoming angrier, his eyes cutting toward me now and again. Sibyl leans back on the balls of her feet and huffs in annoyance, and that's when he snaps.

"Okay, it's obvious that this is all bullshit, and I don't know why I bothered entertaining you. This is some crap you made up to try and shift the blame, and you somehow managed to brainwash her into believing you!" he says, gesturing toward Sibyl, who's still looking.

"Why is it so hard to believe that there's a man out there killing people?" I counter.

"And I'm looking at him! The police saw *no* evidence of another person out there, and we all know it wasn't some fucking bear!"

"You don't know what I saw or what happened!"

"Oh, everyone in town fucking knows what you *saw*. The cops constantly talk about the schizo shit because that's all they see you as: a joke. They know you did it; they just got their hands tied with legal crap and technicalities."

"Oh yeah, an appropriate tone for someone in the future of criminology. Must be so difficult with legal restrictions meant to ensure a fair conviction is in place."

"And you know that many criminals got away with their crimes because of it."

By this time, we're both standing in front of each other, both of us ready to start throwing hands. The air between us is charged, and my chest is already starting to heave as I anticipate the next move, no doubt another punch to my jaw.

"Found it!"

Sibyl's sudden voice pulls our attention away from each other, and we see her holding up the familiar pocket watch. I move to her side, take it from her, and run my fingers over the engraving.

L.B.

"This is it. This is his pocket watch," I mutter before trying to open it. Unfortunately, it's jammed or something because it doesn't budge, and I can't help but think about what's inside. Maybe a cryptic picture of the Man when he was more human. Maybe a picture of an old house, his house, and finding it can lead to more evidence about him.

Or maybe there's nothing inside at all.

I have to open this.

"So, this is your silver bullet? Some old ass watch you can't even open?" Austin scoffs.

"You knew what we were looking for so what's with the skepticism now that we found it? We dreamt about this watch that belongs to the killer, and it's in the exact place we said it would be," I tell him. He rolls his eyes and crosses his arms.

"And how do I know you didn't plant this earlier and put it on a song and dance to try and paint this picture of a madman on the loose?"

"My God, how delusional are you?" I scream at him, my eyes searching his for any sign that he's joking but find nothing. This jackass is serious.

"Bold choice of words. Look, I just find it ridiculous that you're swearing up and down that some supernatural man that only *you* saw is going around randomly killing people, and your only evidence *tangible* is a fucking pocket watch!"

"Hey, I saw him, too!" Sibyl pipes in, glaring at him. He laughs and then gestures to her.

"And don't even get me started on the fact that you're dragging innocent people into your delusions. You're fucking sick, man," Austin says as he starts walking around. "So, so, *so* sick. And the messed-up thing is; I don't think you even know it. I'm starting to think you believe in your crap."

"Where the hell are you going with this now?" I shove the pocket watch in my pocket and pull my arm away when Sibyl grabs it.

"This is going in the exact direction you should've expected. You're guilty and, whether intentionally or not, you're shifting blame. You're so delusional that I have to loop everything I say, keep telling you that there is no smiling man or what-the-fuck-ever you wanna call him and that the only logical suspect is you, Chance."

"You just have everything figured out, huh?"

"No, just you."

We continue to lock eyes as his words hang in there, and I'm left stewing. How dare he? How could he have the audacity to act like he knows me? That he knows what happened that night? That anyone in this fucking town knows what happened that night?

"You don't know a damn thing about me," I tell him, my voice low and steady.

Before he can respond, a phone goes off, and the three of us look at each other for a second until Austin digs into his jacket's pocket. He pulls it out, and his whole demeanor softens before answering it.

"Cyrus? What's-"

"Austin, please help!" A terrified voice cries out.

****

"Cyrus! Cy, where are you? Cy!" Austin cups his hands around his mouth, yelling as loud as he can.

We finally get to the woods, and Austin barely remembers to put the car in park before darting beyond the tree line. Almost immediately, we're out in the woods looking for Cyrus. Thankfully, we decide to stick together considering how dark it is and it seems like it gets even darker inside the woods.

"Are you sure we shouldn't split up? This forest is huge, and it'll take forever to find him, especially when we can't even see what's in front of us," Sibyl says.

"Weren't you two the ones talking about some drunken, dancing, homicidal dude roaming around?" Austin says and scoffs loudly.

Sibyl cuts her eyes towards him, and I can only shake my head. I wonder if having to interact with him finally quenched her thirst.

My eyes drift to a random dirt path that's so obscure that you would miss it if you weren't looking for it. I find myself walking down the path and realize that I can't see or hear the others anymore. Regardless, I continue down the path and a sense of déjà vu washes over me.

I've been down here before, and it's on the tip of my tongue. Every tree I pass brings me closer and closer to a realization when I see someone run in front of me. They're wearing the shirt all the guides have to wear, so I follow after them, somehow being able to follow perfectly but only ever catching glimpses of the person's back.

I stumble as it finally hits me why all of this seems familiar – this is the same path I took during the tour when I was running from the Man. I tripped over this stone, that branch hit my head, I scraped my palms on that tree trunk, and here is where I slid and almost fell in that ditch.

And just like in my memory, I'm led into the same clearing where the world is put on mute; no insects, no birds, just… complete silence. Hell, you can barely hear your heartbeat.

I walk slowly through the clearing, looking around for any clues. Then, I hear the first sound since coming in here in the form of a snapped twig.

Out of the corner of my eye, I spot a figure emerging from the tree line. Just as I'm about to look, a hand grips mine tightly and pulls me to the ground. Before I can open my mouth, a dirty hand covers my mouth, and I look into fearful gray eyes.

****

I always imagined that I would've been a bit happier seeing him looking this scared. Also imagined it would be in a different setting… like a police station with his mom looming over him in disappointment. This is a bit more… bloody than I was expecting. Certainly, didn't expect to be right there with him either.

Cyrus and I are facing each other as we lay on our stomachs, eyes never straying as we listen out for the soft footsteps around us. I move a bit closer and keep my voice as quiet as possible.

"What the fuck are you doing here?"

"I was doing this foreign concept called hanging with my friends," he spits. I roll my eyes, resisting the urge to hit him in the face.

"I swear on everything, I would jump to my feet and call that freak over here. At this point, I couldn't give any less of a fuck about my life let alone yours."

"Okay, okay! Calm down, you psychopath!" He harshly whispers, eyes wide and darting to me and the clearing. "My friends and I were just hanging out like I said when we saw that freak dancing around. We started fucking around with him because he was ignoring us at first before he just suddenly flipped and started running after us. We ran and got separated."

"Why the hell would you antagonize a stranger in the woods?"

"We were just having fun!"

"You little shits are one 'It was just a prank, bro' away from being the standard jackass you would expect from this generation."

"Oh wow, shocker; the millennial has a problem with my generation."

We glare at each other before a twig snaps close by, and we both snap our attention towards it. The Man continues to dance in a wide circle, but I notice that He lingers at certain spots. I crawl forward a bit and note the places: a gnarled tree, He always seems to go there, a mound of snow that seems more conspicuous than any other pile of snow, a tree that seems to have something on it, and He keeps brushing up against a different tree. I want to go check it out closer, but when I move, I feel a hand grip my shirt. Looking back, I see Cyrus looking at me with wide, watery eyes, confusion marring his childish face.

Reluctantly, I move back to my previous position and wait until the Man leaves the area.

"Alright, let's go," I mutter to him before pulling him up.

We run as fast as we can, hoping that the random direction we're going is the way back to the road. Even if it isn't, it's a good enough decision considering any direction away from that freak is the right choice.

It's not surprising that we end up further in the woods, but the silver lining is that we see Austin and Sibyl. But I quickly notice that there's blood coating their clothes, and their eyes are wide as they stare at us. I pull us to a sharp stop and stretch my arm out in front of Cyrus, but he scoffs and shoves it away.

"Why the hell are you two covered in blood?"

They look at each other as if just realizing that their shirts are drenched in blood, their hair dripping with it, and some of it splatters across their face. They look like they just came off the set of some B-rated hack-and-slash movie.

With that in mind, I pull Cyrus back causing him to stumble.

"Dude, chill! My brother isn't dangerous," he scoffs before turning back to them. "Did you find Dylan, Gigi, Zander, or Natalia?"

"Well, we found *some* bodies in a clearing; maybe three?" Sibyl starts.

"Maybe? What's a maybe? You either found my friends or not!" Cyrus spits, glaring at them as his shoulders tremble.

"It's not that simple, Cyrus," Austin lowers his voice to a whisper. One look at Cyrus' face and I can tell that he's getting as pissed and annoyed as I am with his pussyfooting. Austin probably catches on and sighs deeply. "We found three heads, but the bodies were completely mutilated. The heads were the only thing intact."

"What the fuck man?" Cyrus whimpers. Austin takes a step towards him but stops when his eyes glance down at his arms. He takes two steps back and looks at Cyrus with heavy eyes.

"I know this isn't what you want to hear, but… I'm glad none of them were you," he says. His voice is low, and his eyes shine with a familiar gleam.

It's the same look Hawthorne used to throw my way whenever I would run to him after the older kids would pick on me or whenever I would come back home after one of my impromptu adventures through the woods.

A bitter taste enters my mouth before I squash it down, focusing my attention on the disheveled Sibyl whose watery green eyes remain firmly on the ground. Unable to keep my feet from shuffling from foot to foot, I take a few steps closer to her, my hand hovering over her shoulder. Suddenly, her arms are wrapped tightly around my waist, and I cringe back before loosely returning it.

I wonder if I should be worried that the smell of blood doesn't bother me anymore. Doesn't seem like the kind of thing you should get used to.

I bury that thought for another day and look over her head, making eye contact with Austin. For once, it seems that we're on the same page as we usher the others back to the road. The ride back is quiet except for the soft reassurances coming from the backseat as Cyrus struggles to muffle his sobs. I glance at Sibyl who's sitting in a daze with her head lying against the window.

I watch her for a few more minutes, glancing now and again back at the road, but she never looks up. Her arms cross over her stomach, and she softly sniffles. Should I say something? Offer her reassurance? Tell her lies like everything's going to be okay?

"He's not going to stop, is he?" Her voice is barely above a whisper and cracks in the middle of her question.

Instead of responding, I squeeze her hand.

It's a long way home.

Chapter 9

Austin comes out of the bathroom, rubbing his damp hair with a hand towel as he joins the rest of us in the living room. Everyone had wanted to wash the dirt, grime, and blood off of themselves, and the only option was putting on clothes from my closet. I have to force down the irritation I feel when I catch a glance at the number 07 on the old ice hockey jersey and instead refocus on Sibyl.

She's wearing my old high school basketball jersey and my smallest pair of sweats, the drawstrings tied. Her red, puffy eyes don't stray from the empty mug in front of her.

"So, what now?" Cyrus grumbles from his spot.

He's sitting next to me on the couch while Sibyl sits on the loveseat across from us. The smallest graphic tee I own hangs from his frame, but I can tell his focus is on his chipped black nail polish as he picks at it.

"Now, we get all of our stories straight and try to piece this puzzle together. Cyrus, tell us *exactly* what happened before and during your time in the woods," I say, looking at the teen.

"Like I told you earlier, we were just in the woods playing around. It was me, Dylan, Zander, Gigi, and Natalia in the woods, and Dylan was showing us something with his lighter," he starts.

"What the hell did he have to show you with his lighter that required all of you to be in the middle of the woods?" I ask, and he looks at me in annoyance.

"Can I finish?"

And just like that, I'm reminded why I hate teens.

"Anyway, after a couple of hours out there, that guy showed up, and we just thought he was some drunk bum. So, we decided to fuck with him a bit; nothing serious. He didn't do anything, just kept moving around like he was looking for something. I guess we got cocky 'cause he wasn't doing shit, and Gigi started tossing rocks in his direction. One of them hits his head and shit just hit the fan. He was in front of us in, like, a fucking second and ripped her arm off like some deranged kid torturing an insect. Needless to say, we got the fuck outta there.

I don't know where the others went, but I could still hear Gigi screaming. It was… so fucking terrifying. You know those videos on YouTube where commentators would talk about someone's last moments and play their last known audio? When the victim could be heard screaming, and it's the most blood-chilling sound to ever exist? It's so fucked to think that some asshole in his basement is probably going to casually talk about their deaths just to get some clicks on the internet. They don't deserve that and they didn't deserve what happened," Cyrus goes quiet, his eyes staring ahead at nothing.

It's an expression I know all too well, and I avert my gaze when he starts to blink fast.

Austin makes some kind of noise under his breath, and I can't tell if it's one of dissatisfaction or discomfort. Maybe a mix of both?

"What about you two?" Cyrus and I look toward them but a glance at a still-shaken Sibyl has my gaze falling more on Austin. It seems like he got the same idea as he stands behind the couch and grips the back of it.

"After you ran off, we continued looking for Cyrus before we heard some deep growling that freaked us out. It sounded like a wolf, and we were worried that a pack was nearby. We tried losing them but realized that they were herding us somewhere," he explains. I raise an eyebrow, and he continues. "Once we got closer to some clearing, the growling just stopped altogether. That's when we saw the bodies."

Cyrus flinches and curls in on himself and Austin immediately stops talking. My attention falls on Sibyl when she leans forward, her arms resting on her lap.

"As we said earlier, we couldn't tell you if they were all of your friends because we only found three heads and even they were undistinguishable; we couldn't tell you which were male or female. Hell, they could've been some randos the Grinning Man killed earlier. We never found another head."

It goes quiet after that, and Austin moves from his spot behind Sibyl to Cyrus to comfort him, only for the teen to shake the hand off of him. I swallow back the words I want to say, to tell, and just move to the spot beside Sibyl.

"What about you?"

It takes a few seconds to register the question, and when I do, I look up to see Austin watching me.

"What?"

"I mean, what happened to you? You said we have to get all of our stories together to solve this, so what's your story?"

"You guys already know what happened. I wandered off and found Cyrus."

The aforementioned boy rolls his eyes hard and scoffs harshly.

"He means what happened on the tour. You know, the one where our dad died?" he spits, glaring at me. My jaw clenches hard, and, again, I have to swallow back everything I want to say.

He was four feet away from the Grinning Man, his father's actual killer; why the fuck is he looking at me like that?

"He's got a point," a soft voice piped up beside me. Sibyl looks up from her lap, and we make eye contact. Her expression is soft and cautious, and I feel like a small, wounded animal under her gaze.

I don't want to.

I don't want to think about the dreams – memories – that have been plaguing my mind, but we're so close to the finish line that maybe… it's needed for the last hurdle.

"Well, as you know, the tour happened last year, and I don't think I need to go into specifics, right? Everybody in the group died except for me, and for a year, I couldn't remember what exactly happened until a detective showed me the pictures. They were… brutal. Seriously, you don't want specifics. Just know that there's a reason why I've been so terrified of him.

Anyway, I recently started having dreams, o-or rather memories, of the incident before they escalated into encounters solely with the Grinning Man. They always showed different things but the common feature is that He's always either looking for something or talking to me directly. I never wanted to hear what he had to say, but I started listening to see if I could get some clues on what he wanted or even why he did what he did. Instead, all he talked about was not wanting to harm me and just wanting to talk.

Now, I've been trying to connect the evidence I got from the visions like locations, items, and what he says. So far, all I know is that whatever he's looking for is in the woods, and he'll kill anyone who gets in the way of that. Also, I think he has some kind of pet dog. I kept seeing deep claw marks around my house, constant howling, and clumps of black fur; they especially appeared around His locations. Not only that but a couple of victims looked like they were torn apart by an animal. He's out there killing, and He has a pet contributing to those kills."

It's quiet for a minute as they look at each other, and I can see Cyrus clenching his fists in his lap, his head tilted forward and long fringe covering his eyes.

"What happened to our dad, specifically?" Cyrus mutters. This draws a wince outta me.

"C'mon, don't do this to yourself. You don't want that."

"DON'T TELL ME WHAT I WANT!" he screams. His eyes are wide as he glares down at me, and I can see Austin standing behind him, looking like he's stuck between pulling him back and forcing me to answer himself.

I take a breath and run my fingers through my hair.

"When we got separated from the rest of the group, your dad, Jacob, was trying to save everyone, anyone. When that didn't work, he tried to, at least, keep me safe. He was dragging me along so I wouldn't fall behind until something tackled him and knocked me down a hill," I trail off for a second, but I can't bring myself to look at either of their faces. "His head was thrown in front of where I was hiding."

"And his body?"

"Never saw it, but based on the condition the others were found in, it's probably for the best. Trust me on that."

Cyrus stands abruptly and walks to the corner of the room, and I force myself to keep eye contact with Austin. The brown color brightens with the watery sheen now in them, and he looks away first.

"Why would He do that?" The raw horror in Sibyl's voice is a sound I'm familiar with, a sound that I've heard many times coming from myself.

"I've been asking myself that every day for a year."

"You should've died on that tour."

The voice comes quietly, and, for a second, I think I might've said my thoughts out loud until Sibyl jumps to her feet, glaring at Austin.

"What the hell, Austin?" she screams. "Why would you say that?"

"You should've died," he continues. "Why did my dad have to die? Why were you spared?"

"Another thing I kept asking myself. Why me? Why not the loving father? Why not the elderly couple? Why not the young man begging for his mom? Why not the fucking teen who had her entire life ahead of her? I don't know, Austin, okay? *I don't know*," I stress.

He watches me for a few good minutes and finally lowers his eyes to his lap, and, for once, I feel something other than annoyance or anger towards him.

Suddenly, I hear the snow crunching and graveling moving in my driveway, and in one smooth motion, Austin is standing in front of Cyrus and Sibyl, and I stand off to the side. Austin and I share a look, and I move slowly toward the door, slightly lift the blinds, and look to the front door.

"Fucking Isolde," I mutter before throwing the door open. It takes a minute to register what I'm seeing and even longer to recognize this disheveled figure is Isolde.

I've never seen her with her hair out of place, and yet here she is: baggy clothes, no make-up, and the usual scent of green apple and blackberries completely absent from her body and hair. A twinge of discomfort nibbles at me and has me shuffling on my feet.

Don't forget that she left your ass out to drown.

"What the hell do you want, Isolde?"

"You haven't been any of your appointments lately," she says.

I wince when her voice cracks painfully in the middle, and it's only then that I notice how cracked her lips are, beads of blood resting on them.

"Seriously? Does it look like I'm worried about some fucking appointments?" I scoff and cross my arms over my chest. "Sorry, I've been busy."

"Busy with what? Running around town with the guy that keeps assaulting you or my assistant who should be doing her job instead of encouraging your delusions?"

"You mean the assistant that's done more for me in the few weeks that I've known her than you've ever done in the years that I've known you?" Her eyes become dimmer but that's all that happens. "And don't worry about what I'm doing with Austin. He might be an ass, but at least I expect it from him. What you did was some shady shit."

I feel someone behind me and glance back to see Sibyl and Austin; both of their bodies taut and eyes narrowed.

"Ms. Ashford, I'm, like, really sorry that I haven't been working lately, but Chance needed my help," Sibyl starts, an awkward smile on her lips. "Besides, I'm preeeeetty sure I got some vacation time saved up."

The blank gaze Isolde levels on Sibyl unsettles me enough to have me shuffling between them. However, her relentless stare sets off warning bells in my head as it feels like she's looking right through me.

"Do you think you have the right to try and pull this crap after what you did? Or were you just hoping that I magically forgot that you *lied* to the fucking police? I could've been jailed *for life*, and the fact that you can't even *pretend* to offer up a half-assed apology speaks volumes about the kind of person you are!"

Her dull eyes lazily drift back to me, and she takes so long to respond, that I start to wonder if she's on something. With the way she looks, it doesn't seem too far off.

"And the fact that you didn't think of how that would've impacted me shows what kind of person you are," she says. Her voice is quiet and full of venom.

"What the hell are you talking about?"

"Did it ever even cross your mind that if people found out about us, I could lose my job, my reputation? No one is going to hire a psychologist who's fucking their patient."

"But you weren't thinking of that when you were sucking my dick, were you?"

SLAP!

I look at the wall as my face burns from the sharp impact. Sibyl gasps loudly, but, other than that, no one makes a sound.

Annoyance and anger fester inside my chest, and I have to take a few deep breaths, close my eyes, and turn my head back to Isolde. She still has that dead expression on her face, but her eyes seem to have gained that familiar gleam.

"Don't talk to me like that," she says, her voice low and strained.

"But am I wrong?" I ask, my voice matching hers. "Isolde, don't forget that you initiated this relationship, you kept pushing for it to continue, and you're the one who, after doing all that shit, was perfectly fine throwing me to the sharks just to protect your reputation. Even if it meant me sitting on death row."

Exhaustion wears down on her, and she shakes her head in what seems like resignation and disappointment.

"We don't have time for this," she mutters. "We can talk about this in the car, but we need to go now."

"Just wait one goddamn second, Bettie Page. We got more important shit to worry about than you getting dicked down," Cyrus scoffs. The small yelp and quiet hiss of his name almost catches my attention, but I manage to keep my eyes on her.

"I'm not going with you, Isolde."

"You are," she stresses.

"*No*, I'm not."

"Let me rephrase this in a way you can understand," she mutters, and I huff as I'm forced to strain my ears just to hear her. "You either come with me or I'll have you institutionalized."

Whatever retort I'm about to say gets caught in my throat, and a hard shiver runs through my body. I want to call her out on her bluff, to see any sign of weakness that could tell me she wouldn't, *couldn't* follow through with her threat, but I find none.

"And you call him the crazy one," Cyrus says and scoffs.

"Ms. Ashford, you can't do that!"

"Sibyl, I don't want to hear anything from you, traitor," Isolde spits.

"But she's right. You're going to wrongfully institutionalize someone just because they don't want to be with you?" Austin chimes in as he moves to my side. "You said it yourself; if people found out you were hooking up with your patient, your reputation would go up in flames. Imagine the reception you'd get if they found out the reason why you got him locked up. They'll eat you alive."

"That's something I'm willing to risk," she says and turns to look me in the eyes. "Now, get in the car."

****

The tension in the car is palpable, and I take advantage of her unsettling intense focus on the road to inspect her more closely. Her white shirt softly reflects the moonlight, but the shirt is wrinkled, her dark jeans are scruffy, and her off-white shoes are worn out.

However, her outfit isn't what catches my attention but rather her arms. With an eerie sense of familiarity, I register the deep, red scratches all over her arms as if she clawed at them in a desperate attempt to get something from underneath her skin in a state of paranoia.

The old scratches on my arm burn, so I turn my attention to anything else I can see on her.

There are dark, heavy bags under her bloodshot eyes, her pupils are blown wide to the point where I wonder if she's on something, her body softly trembles with the occasional harsh shudder that wracks through her completely, and her leg bounces with manic energy. Honestly, the more I see, the more uneasy I feel.

"Izzy?"

It's as if she can't hear me as she doesn't move an inch or even blink.

What catches my attention, though, is the bead of some mysterious liquid trailing down her ear. It trickles down her jawline, hangs on her chin, and drops. A few more follow that trail until a steady stream forms, but Isolde doesn't snap out of her daze. I flinch when that black, blood-like substance starts to slowly trickle from her bloodshot eyes. It's producing a putrid smell that has me gagging.

"Isolde, you need to go to the hospital," I say, trying to keep my voice soft. The last thing I need is to agitate her into crashing or something. "Isolde, please listen to me for one second! You have to-"

"Did you ever love me?"

The question bounces in my mind for a second, and the curveball disorients me for a minute. I wait for her to elaborate, to give me anything I could work with, or, at least, something that pertains to my concerns. But I get nothing.

"What?"

"I had a dream last night, Chance. Do you wanna know what it was?"

The blood is now pouring out, becoming darker and darker until it looks completely black. The smell turns from fishy to rancid meat, and my mouth starts quickly and repeatedly filling with saliva as my stomach turns.

"Izzy, please, l-let's just pull over and talk," I beg her.

"I saw a tall Man wearing a suit. He was dancing on the sidewalk, and I was so scared that I couldn't even move. When he noticed me, he started walking in this exaggerated tiptoe manner like he was in some old cartoon. I finally forced myself to move to the other side of the sidewalk and when I looked back at him, he was facing my direction with one foot raised in the air… like he was about to take a step but froze when I looked at him."

Tears fall down her face, mixing with the black blood.

"I was so scared, Chance. So fucking scared. I mean, who does that? What kind of monster makes a game out of tormenting people?"

"Izzy…"

"I tried to run, but he caught me, Chance. He caught me. I screamed for you, but you never came. Why didn't you help me? I thought you loved me, so why didn't you *help*?" Her voice cracks as her trembling hands tightly grip the wheel. Tears are streaming down both of our faces and after swallowing past the painful lump in my throat, I move to comfort her. As I'm turning my body, my eyes catch on to a straw doll in the backseat.

Isolde's behavior has me on edge, but it's the sight of this doll that leaves me feeling like I fell headfirst into the chilly depths of the ocean with all of the dread of seeing the vast amount of nothingness in front of me.

Sudden shrieking startles me, and I realize that I have been reaching for the doll, prompting Isolde to start going crazy. With both hands off the wheel, she starts to strike me as hard as she can, I have to endure it and steer the car as it moves erratically on the road.

"Izzy, what the hell are you doing?" I scream at her, jerking the wheel again when it hits the rumble strips.

"Don't touch, it's mine!" Her voice comes out hoarse and aggressive with no trace of the woman I know left in her. A sharp punch hits my face, and a cracking sound fills my ears before blood gushes down into my mouth.

"Izzy, we're going to crash!"

"Why are you doing this to me!?"

"I'm not doing anything! The Grinning Man is playing with your head! You gotta snap out of it!"

"Don't touch that! Don't touch, don't touch, don't touch, don't touch!"

Now, I know that this doll has some sort of dark hold on her and taking it will only further agitate her. But something is compelling me to take it, and I momentarily let go of the wheel and lunge backward to snatch up the doll. Before I can even attempt to get back to the wheel, an ear-piercing, inhuman shriek fills the car.

It catches me so off-guard that stabilizing the car didn't even cross my mind as I desperately clutch at my ears, a muted ringing resonating through my head.

The next thing I know, my stomach drops as I'm suspended in the air for a minute too long before being thrown around violently as the car lands heavily and begins to flip. We're forced to a harsh stop when my side hits something, and my head smashes against the window, stunning me.

My eyes and chest feel heavy, and I sluggishly bring my hand up to my head. Looking at the blood now coating my fingers, I grow more and more lightheaded before… nothing.

****

I'm by the road. Why?

Looking around and checking my body, I can't come up with any answer as to why I'm here instead of back in the car. The only thing I can do is wait.

Wait for the Man to appear like always.

And when he finally does, all I can do is look at his impeccable, never-changing appearance as he towers over me. My heart, strangely enough, remains steady.

"What do you want now? And what did you do to Isolde?"

"Isolde?" He tilts his head curiously to the left. Just like before, His voice only resonates through my mind. "Ah, Ms. Ashford. Quite unfortunate what happened to her. How dreadful."

I can feel my teeth grinding against each other and have to force myself to relax.

"You didn't need to drag her into this shit – she didn't deserve it!"

"Oh, but she was already involved the moment she met you. But, enough of that! We have work to do, so you must awaken."

I grab his arm as he makes a move backward, and the stare he gives me sends chills down my spine. It has me removing my hold and moving back.

"Please, leave her-"

"Time's a-wasting!"

A screech is what pulls me from unconsciousness, and my body aches from my sudden movement. A cursory glance over my body reveals several spots on my arms and torso, no doubt going to form into bruises later, my right arm has a deep purple bruise along with a small lump that I soon identified as a bone out of place and threatening to break through my skin, and a throbbing pain behind my eyes accompanies my concussion.

I grunt as I attempt to move again.

Isolde.

Looking at the driver's side, the door is almost completely ripped from its hinges, and the airbag has already flattened. After ripping my seatbelt off, I practically throw myself into the driver's seat, pulling myself out with the support of the barely hanging door, and haul myself to the ground.

"Fuck."

Pressing against a deep cut on my forehead, I pull myself to my feet.

"Isolde! Izzy, are you okay? Where are you?" I scream, my voice raspy, and I start coughing harshly. A spine-tingling scream rings out from the woods, and my feet move faster than my mind toward it.

Before I can reach the screaming, He interrupts me, and I barely have time to avoid crashing into Him and, instead, fall backward. The pain doesn't even register as I stare up at Him. Despite Him always having that disturbing grin on his face, I had never once felt any "happy" vibes from Him until this moment.

Why the fuck is He so happy? That He finally caught me? That we're finally face-to-face?

"What the fuck did you do with Isolde?"

I don't even recognize my voice, but it doesn't matter as He only tilts His head curiously. A low humming noise reaches my ears, and it takes a moment to realize it's coming from His throat.

Or… at least, it's supposed to. Just like with His voice, it sounds more like it's coming through an old-timey radio that I can only hear in my head. It's hard to tell if it's pleasant or not; there's something hypnotic yet disturbing about it.

"Are you going to answer me or just keep standing there like a jackass?"

Why are you antagonizing him?

"Why not just hurry up and kill me? Why the pussyfooting?"

Shut up.

"Or do you need me to do everything for you?"

Seriously, what the fuck are you doing!?

"And what's up with that mutt of yours? Do I even wanna know why you constantly have him following you around, you freak?"

You fucking idiot!

"Hey! Say something! What the fuck-"

In one swift, smooth motion, He pulls me up, grabs my waist to pull me closer, and begins to do that drunken waltz He seems to love so much.

I'm stumbling over my feet and trying to calm my pounding heart from the sudden movement. I try pulling from His grasp, but his hold doesn't falter as He continues His fucked foxtrot.

"Why the long face? We should be celebrating!"

An ear-grating noise fills my head, and I soon realize it's His version of laughing.

I renew my struggles and when I feel one of his hands loosen, it gives me the chance to completely pull away. With that, I run toward the only place I can think of – the woods.

I had forgotten about the screaming from before until I hit the tree lines, and a choked gurgle caught my attention. There, I see Isolde.

My knees hit the ground hard, but it doesn't register as all I can do is look at her barely heaving chest before wincing as I can hear disturbing rattles coming deep from her throat. She makes for a bloody painting, and the most gruesome subjects in the image are the long gash across her stomach that's spilling her guts, and her chest is cracked open like a carved Thanksgiving turkey.

Yes, her chest was wide open.

The grisly injury gives me a clear look inside her slowly beating heart, and it squirts up blood like a ground spray on a splash pad.

"Help… me," she says, her voice weak. My hands hover over her body before I have to shove them in my lap, clenching my jeans, in hopes of restraining myself.

"Fuck, Izzy," I mutter. Her eyes lazily roam with no destination before settling on my face but are still glazed over. "Izzy, can you say anything?"

Her head barely shakes, and I push her hand down as she shakily brings it up. Her lips move, and I have to lean in to try and hear.

"Help… me."

"How? Y-you're bleeding too much."

"Help… help…" her words get quieter and quieter until I can't hear her anymore no matter how close I get.

My mind blanks, and I start to tourniquet her torso with my jacket like that would do shit. Movement out the corner of my eye catches my attention, and, to my horror, I spot the Grinning Man standing nearby, His head tilted to the side.

"Don't… leave… help."

His head tilts to the other side.

"… love… you."

He takes a step forward, and I move to my feet.

"Stay… me…"

Another step forward and a matching one back.

"P-please… love… you…"

His Grin widens, and He takes another mocking step. A weak tug causes me to look down into Isolde's teary eyes.

"Kill… me… kill… me."

Without another look back, I run inside the woods, Isolde's weak voice ringing in my head.

Chapter 10

Help me!

Help me!

Kill me!

The pleas keep bouncing around in my mind, and the image of Isolde's body is imprinted in my mind.

Why? Why did I run away? Why didn't I help her!? Was it out of spite? Was it my cowardice once again overriding my morals?

You know why.

Bile rises in my throat. What did Isolde do to deserve this? Try to help me through all of my shitty problems? Stick her neck out to show me the first positive human interaction since the whole town turned its back on me? Risk her life and career just for some half-assed affection from a guy who doesn't have any of his shit together?

For fucking loving me?

No, the answer is she did shit all to deserve this. Her only sin was that she was stupid enough to get close to me because *everyone* who does ends up suffering.

Before I can wallow any further in my self-pity, someone tackles me, and I almost hit the ground if it wasn't for them yanking me toward them. They pull me upright, and we start running in a different direction. I finally realize that it's Austin, and his eyes are wide and constantly darting in everywhere direction.

"What are you doing here?"

He doesn't answer; he just pulls me harder and forces me to run faster.

"Austin!"

"Shut up! Just shut up and keep moving!"

We finally stop to catch our breath and I have to lean against a tree as a wave of nausea hits me hard. Austin continues to look around, his shoulders tense and constantly shuffling on the spot. I have to call his name a few times before his body flinches backward, and he finally looks at me. Repressing the memory of Isolde's body, I try to think of the possible cause of Austin's erratic behavior. I swallow hard to regain my breath, a heavy weight on my chest that has me swaying on my feet.

That or it's all the blood I lost.

"What's wrong? D-Did you run into the Grinning Man?"

"We got bigger problems."

"Bigger than a homicidal alien?" I scoff before I faintly hear something in the distance. I have to strain to hear what sounds like dogs barking. "What the hell is that?"

"The bigger problem. When we got in my car to follow after you guys, we saw a shit ton of police passing by. We followed them and hid when they had stopped by the totaled car. There, we heard them talking on the radio," he explains, and I can hear my heart pounding in my chest. "They found the teens' bodies and suspect you did it. Them finding Isolde's car and body solidified it."

"Fuck." I run my fingers through my hair, and the sound of dogs gets closer to our location, causing both of us to tense. Without wasting another second, we run in the direction further from the noise. Before we can get far, I pull us in yet another direction after spotting the Grinning Man dancing not too far from our location. Not only that, but I can also faintly hear the sound of a low, haunting growl that can only belong to the wolf by the Grinning Man's side, and I can't even locate where he is.

And just like that, we're running from threats on all sides.

I can't speak for him, but I'm just running blindly, praying that we won't run into any of them. I don't even know where we're running to or even what the end game is; am I just going to keep running the rest of my life? Forever looking over my shoulder until I can't take anymore and decide to just opt out?

A sharp yank pulls me to the side, and I glance to the side to see some light beams heading our way and start picking up my pace. Austin's tight grip on my good arm is the only thing I can focus on as I try to shake off the lightheadedness that continues to creep up and has me tripping over almost everything. The shouts from the cops, demanding us to stop running, but it might as well be white noise as black spots form in my peripherals.

My head lobs to one side, and I almost choke on my sharp inhale when realizing that He got a lot closer than before and gaining on us. We lock eyes for a minute and I make a decision.

"What-!"

Austin stumbles after I push him away, and I don't stick around to hear any protests, running in the opposite direction of him but heading down a path close to Him.

I see Him take the bait and follow after me. Burning pain flares up every time my shoulder shifts, I can barely see in front of me as blood keeps dripping into my eyes, and the slightest hip movement has my eyes and body burning.

I glance over my shoulder and see Him running swiftly, arms pumping and catching up quickly. His head lolls a bit until we make direct eye contact.

"That's right! Come and get me, you fucker!" I rasp out, my voice cracking a bit.

My feet almost slip under me when I hit a patch of mud, but I right myself just in time to avoid the large, thin hand that almost grabs my bad shoulder. I push myself harder and faster, and I swear I can hear him laugh inside my head. After taking a few hard lefts and sharp rights, I feel like I might've lost him.

Pain explodes in the side of my face, and blood fills my mouth after something solid hits me. The snow beneath me spreads a numbing cold all over my body, and it takes a minute for everything to stop spinning.

Click.

****

Hollow.

After the initial shock wears off, that's the only thing I can use to describe what I'm feeling as I look up into the barrel of a gun, and behind it is a furious brunette female who's holding it steady as she levels a stone-cold glare on me. My eyes drift to the side at the two large German Shepherds that are practically foaming at the mouth with their ears pinned back and occasionally mock charging towards me.

Slowly under her stare, I rise to my feet, and her grip tightens on her gun.

"Put your hands up!" she orders.

"Please, listen. You're in danger-"

"I said put your hands up now! Where I can see them!"

I huff and slowly raise my arms until they're beside my head, the hot pain radiating from my right arm has my mind going blank until the growling captures it again. It feels like there's cotton in my mouth, and I have to swallow through it to continue.

"Listen, the real killer is out here right now, and he'll kill again if we don't-"

"Get down on your knees-"

"If we don't do something now, he's going to catch up-"

"Sir, if you continue to not cooperate, I can and *will* use force. It's in your best interest to *get on the fucking ground!*"

I slowly drop to my knees, press my chest on the ground, and place my hands behind my head. The dogs move closer to me to the point that I can smell their breath and feel their saliva dripping on my neck. The anger rumbling from their chest promises a slow and painful end, and I can practically feel the canines sinking themselves in my neck.

"You're making a mistake," I try again, but I already know it's too late.

The dogs are no longer growling and instead, they are pacing around us. When I attempt to raise my head, she's quick to demand I put it back down, which I quickly do.

"I didn't kill anyone; I was trying to find the person who did." She scoffs and starts approaching me, the gun most definitely still trained on me.

"Funny. I think Bundy said the same thing," she says. However, my focus is on the noises the dogs are making…or rather, lack of. And that's when I heard it.

Aggressive barking, scared whimpers, and finally, pained yelps.

"What the fuck?" the officer screams, and I can just barely see her feet as she whips around. I keep my face on the ground and curl in tighter as that familiar feeling of cold dread shoots down my spine.

"Hey, you! Freeze, don't come any closer!"

My heart starts to pound even harder, and my flight-or-fight instincts decide to go with freeze.

"Sir, if you keep approaching, I will shoot! This is your last- fuck!"

Gunshots ring out like thunder in my ears, causing me to flinch with each one.

One.

Two.

Three.

Four.

She produces the most bloodcurdling scream and the distinguishable sound of bones breaking rings throughout the air before nothing but harsh silence. Fear and a morbid curiosity drive me to finally look up, but the only things there are The

Grinning Man and large blood stains, the officer and dogs nowhere in sight.

I slowly pull myself to my knees, taking in the Man's bloody clothes and limbs, and I wait with bated breath for the next move. But, besides a mockingly innocent head tilt, there was none. Something catches my attention from the corner of my head, and a glance reveals that the officer's gun was dropped. He must've noticed as he takes an exaggerated, cartoonish step toward it.

What kind of monster makes a game out of tormenting people?

A renewed rage has me scrambling toward the gun, and I pick it up, aim it as steadily as I can manage, and unload the rest of the clip into his body. Soon, the only thing I can hear is clicking, but the man is still standing.

"I knew you were some kind of freak," I spit loud enough for him to hear. I can see blood on all of the places I hit, four in his chest, one through his hip, one through his throat, and one through his forehead. This just confirms that he's either some kind of supernatural creature, an alien, or some other fucked up thing.

Right in front of me, I watch as the visible wounds close and push out the bullets.

The air becomes static as he looks at me, his eyes darkening to a discerning degree, and, despite the lack of a shift in expression, something more chaotic and primal shows on his face. After a few more desperate attempts with the gun, I end up throwing it at him and running as fast as I can.

I don't get far before a heavy force slams into my side, sending me hurling against a tree. I gasp and try to suck in as much air as I can, but each time I inhale, my chest constricts painfully. When I fall, I land face-first but quickly scramble to my feet to get away, only for him to grab the back of my shirt and throw me in the air. It feels like I'm in the air for hours before landing painfully on my back. In my new position, I barely catch a glimpse of the Grinning Man when I'm roughly thrown back to the ground. I cough out blood, and pain is the only thing I can register.

Yet, I make sure to look up into his eyes.

I was always meant to die.

My birth (surprising, accidental, a chance – a mistake) should have been my death as my umbilical cord had wrapped around my neck, yet I survived, setting off the course of my life that tried to correct this.

At three years old, I got a high fever that damn near killed me. It turns out the doctors almost didn't catch that I had meningitis.

At five, my mom had some kind of psychotic breakdown and stabbed me – thank God she missed my heart. But I can't help but sometimes wonder if I should be thanking him.

In Fourth grade, I fell into the ice-cold lake in the woods behind my house, my heart stopping for three minutes. Hawthorne breathed his life into mine.

The time when I was 12 and our home was broken into when Hawthorne, Darcy, and Arthur were out. One of the armed men narrowly avoided finding me in my hiding spot. Something in my gut told me he would've pulled the trigger.

Then there was three years ago that I went outside to check out some weird ass animal noises only to discover I would've died from monoxide poisoning from a gas leak I wasn't even aware of.

And now, I'm right back where I've always been... staring death in the face.

And as I'm held in death's hand, a cold thumb pressing against my windpipe, and my eyes looking into death's merciless gaze, I understand his resentment towards me. I keep challenging him, challenging fate, and he's tired of our little back-and-forths.

Nietzsche once said, "And if you gaze long enough into an abyss, the abyss will gaze back into you."

Instead of talking in riddles, he should've just told me straight up that the abyss and I have the same eyes.

Suffocation is a strange thing.

Things become peaceful after the initial struggle for a single breath of air and the chest ache from the lack of oxygen. Once it gets to that stage of lightheadedness, a sort of euphoria takes hold. I kick my legs out, but at this point, I don't even know if it's to get him to let go or hurry him along; all I know is that it does nothing.

Now, for the first time in what feels like forever, we stare at each other, face-to-face.

Chapter 11

His grip tightens for a second, completely cutting off my air before letting me fall to the ground. A harsh wave of coughs wracks my body, and I have to spit out another mouthful of blood before losing all of my strength and falling limply to the side.

I force myself to look at Him; each drag upward is physically painful and mentally draining. When I finally lock eyes with Him, it feels like some of the heat from earlier seems to have cooled some, but there's an obvious warning lurking deep in those dark eyes. I curl into myself to ease some of my pain, but he doesn't move from his spot.

My body tenses when He shifts His weight to the side, but all He does is lift His arm and point to the left. Even as my chest heaves painfully, I follow His movement, and all I see is a gnarled pine tree with a bed of belladonna and oleander flowers at the base. Something is hidden within the bed.

"I hope that we can come to a better understanding, Mr. Curran. Until then, I, unfortunately, must be on my way, but rest assured!" His voice gradually lowers, and the glower returns. *"We will meet again. Ta-ta!"*

He stares for a moment longer, and my heart starts to pound as my eyes lower, looking left and right, taking in every possible escape route. I can feel His presence still looming over me, and I sink lower and lower into the ground the longer He stands there before I finally hear the tell-tale signs of Him walking away.

I harshly wipe my nose and eyes before pushing myself to my feet, almost falling back down a couple of times. I look around to make sure He doesn't come back and can faintly hear crickets softly chirping from the trees.

The noise brings a sense of comfort I've never experienced from something as stupid as some fucking insects, and I wipe at my face again, the snow clinging to my hands and seeping into my skin. At this point, I can't tell if I'm feeling numb because of the cold or if it's just the aftereffects of His presence.

A gleam catches my attention, and I remember that something's inside the flowerbed. When I start pushing the flowers and snow away, I find a woman's boot, a bloodied and torn woman's blouse, a familiar boy's forest green jersey that has the name and number torn from it, and, finally, a golden wedding band with a strange dark green speckled stone with specks of red and gold scattered throughout.

That sick fuck wanted to show off his kills.

I stuff the ring in my pocket and turn my attention back to the tree or, more specifically, the hole in the tree. There's nothing inside that I can see, but the dark stain around it. I chip off some of it before realizing that it's dried blood.

"Fuck…" I stand up, quickly brushing off the flakes from my hands.

"Chance!"

Before I can even look back, arms wrap painfully around my chest and press down harshly on my right arm. Despite this, I melt in Sibyl's embrace, leaning my weight entirely on her as the smell of blood, the outdoors, and toasted coconut fills my nose. Her ginger curls tickle my face before she pulls away and runs her hands over my face. I then notice the deep bite mark on her forearm.

"What happened?"

"We ran into His dog, and it really didn't appreciate me stealing its owner's property."

I can feel my jaw open and close before I can finally choke out a "What?"

Sibyl pulls out an iron knife with some kind of design welded on the blade, a small clay bottle full of some kind of liquid, and a ceramic dog with the tail and one of the upright ears broken. I take the knife and turn it over a few times in my hand.

"Where did you find these things?" I mutter.

"You won't believe it, but when we were looking for you, I got separated from the guys and ended up finding some old cabin. I went inside and found a bunch of crap but could only carry a few things. Then, that dog came outta nowhere, bit me, and chased us out!" Sibyl pouts, and I can't stop the smile from forming. "Then we were literally running for our lives, ran into a few cops that roughed us up before the dog got him, and then it was back to running. It caught up to attack us a couple of times but ended up disappearing."

"Sounds crazy."

"I know, right?! I wish I, like, took a picture or video or something of the whole thing! No one's ever gonna believe me, and it's totally not fair!" She throws her arms in the air but yelps and clutches the injured one.

It's only then that I notice Austin and Cyrus standing behind her, both looking just as banged up as her, if not more. Austin's covered in dirt and grime, has bleeding scratches over his arms, and has a rather deep cut on his forehead that has blood gushing down his face while Cyrus is leaning most of his weight on his right leg, is holding his bloodied side, and has a harsh-looking bruise on the right side of his jaw.

Austin moves to her side, clenches his teeth, and wraps a dirty bandana he seemingly pulls out of nowhere around her wound, and Sibyl's cheeks turn red as she watches him.

"I'm pretty sure that chunk of meat taken out of your arm is proof enough," Cyrus says before huffing in annoyance. Sibyl just pouts again.

"Still would've made a cool video," she mutters.

After he's done, Austin turns to look at me while Sibyl and Cyrus continue to bicker.

"Why did you ditch me when we were running from the cops?"

The other two suddenly turn to me, and all of my injuries seem to flare to life, sending a wave of pain through my body.

"I-I saw the Grinning Man following us and knew that he was after me, so I tried to lure him away," I rub at my right arm, wincing. "Didn't go too well."

"He did that?" Austin gestures to my face, and I'm confused for a split second. "That big ass mark on your jaw."

"O-oh… no, that was from the officer who caught up with me. She struck me across the face with the butt of her gun."

"And then?"

The ground is suddenly more interesting as an uncomfortable silence settles over us, the only noise brave enough to cut through the atmosphere being our labored breathing. Sibyl starts sniffling, and I feel a dull pain in my arm and realize that I was trying to pick at my skin.

"What usually happens?"

"Goddammit!" Cyrus kicks the trunk of a nearby tree, and Austin looks at him quickly.

"Calm down," he orders and turns to look at me. "Do you know where He went?"

I look to the side and shake my head, causing the brothers to scoff harshly.

"After He killed Isolde, He immediately stalked me through the woods. Then, He ate some bullets, killed the cop, and beat my ass. He swore we would meet again then disappeared."

"Fan-fucking-tastic," Austin growls, and Cyrus shakes his head. "How does this fucker keep getting away!? When is this shit going to end?"

No one answers, and Austin drags his hand over his face. I rub my arm, and Sibyl's hold on me tightens when I start to sway on my feet. I have to drag my eyes back to Austin, not realizing that they had closed at some point. It's only then that I notice Sibyl stepping a bit too close to the flowerbed.

"Careful; those oleanders are extremely toxic. You don't want any of those touching your skin."

Sibyl jumps away from me and the flowers, her eyes wide and she starts running her hands through her hair.

"Oh, what the heck! Wait! Did you *touch* them!?"

A smile threatens to slip on my lips, and I have to fight it back when she glares at me.

"Yeah, you definitely gotta wash, like, every inch of your body at least twice," this time, a laugh did escape before I choked it back. "It sounds like I'm joking, but it's actually sound advice. When I say they're toxic, I mean sub-Reddit levels of toxic."

"Ugh! Why were you even touching toxic flowers!?"

"I was looking for some things under that tree, and it seemed worth the risk."

Austin straightens up and looks at the tree, his brows furrowing.

"What's up with the tree? Why the sudden interest?"

"I-I don't know, but something's off with it. There's nothing inside, but He was pointing at it before he left," I explain and show them the stuff I found. Austin takes the jersey while Sibyl checks out the blouse.

"You found all this stuff?" Austin whispers.

"And this is a *cute* blouse!" Sibyl marvels. "You know, if you're into the whole *Blair Witch* vibe." She stretches out one of the sleeves, and her eyes actively avoid the blood stains.

"Found everything right at the base. I figured they were His kills."

Cyrus groans in annoyance and anger then pulls out his phone, taking a picture of the tree before snatching the ring from my hand.

"Wherever they came from, I'm gonna find out. I'm going to connect these pieces and finally put an end to that freak," he spits, his eyes darkening as he stares at the ring.

"*We're* going to solve this."

Cyrus cuts his eyes toward me, and I hold contact with him. He huffs and starts walking away. Austin looks at me for a split second and follows after him, the jersey still in his hands. Sibyl tucks the blouse under her arm and places her hand on my shoulder.

"C'mon, Chance. We can figure this out later. For now, let's just go," she says.

Together, we follow after the brothers, and just before I leave, I glance over my shoulder. There, beside the gnarled tree, is a figure kneeling in the flowers. Before I can get a clear view of them, they vanish.

I can't wait to see them up close.

Chapter 12

I can't imagine how fucking crazy we look; the town's psychopath and a ginger chick bloodied and covered in dirt while a bruised-up goth kid messes around on his phone in the corner. It probably doesn't help that the aforementioned ginger keeps fussing with her hair and clothes like it makes a difference with her Scream Queen appearance.

Needless to say, we got a couple of looks from the petty criminals that cops brought in.

We've been waiting in the receptionist's room for hours as the cops, naturally, questioned us about everything. There's a trail of bodies surrounding us after law enforcement was sent to apprehend us, we all look like we got jumped, and there's the fact that I have a rap sheet, despite being proven innocent, and keep being found at crime scenes.

All in all, I'm more surprised they haven't just thrown me in a cell.

The harsh florescent lights crackle, and it snaps my attention to in front of me where an officer roughly leads a struggling man forward, his face set in a deep scowl as he spits obscenities at the woman behind him.

"Just shut up already," she groans, pushing him again when he tries dragging his feet.

She starts talking to the guy behind the desk, and the rowdy man lazily looks around before we make eye contact. His dark eyes scrutinize me for a second before a blank expression falls on his face.

I look at Cyrus and Sibyl, but they're both preoccupied with their own things.

Looking back, I notice the familiar black substance dripping from his eyes, and I can feel my stomach drop as it continues to drip down. No one else pays attention to us, and I swallow hard when his body trembles.

Drip.

Drip.

Drip.

The black substance is now falling behind his back, and his hands are doing something. The officer glances at him and does a double-take, her eyes widening.

"What the hell are you doing!? Someone, get the first aid kit!"

She spins him around to get a better look at his hands, and it's then that he lets black blood-coated fingernails fall to the ground with a sickening plop.

My mouth waters rapidly, and before I can swallow it back, I start vomiting on the ground, sending Cyrus and Sibyl to their feet. Everyone's rushing around, and things get more hectic when he falls to the ground and starts shaking.

"Fuck, he's having a seizure!"

I can't look away from him as his head lolls to the side, and a milky film now covers his eyes as he stares past me. It's like my hearing goes out and all that's left is white noise as officers work on reviving Izzy.

Her dirty blonde is matted with that black gunk and the icy blue eyes that had always looked at me with heat and passion have now been replaced with cold indifference. Black, bloody tears trail down her sunken, pallor cheeks, a drop seeping into her cracked lips.

Desperately, I wait.

I wait to hear the words of blame. I wait for the harsh accusations. I wait for the sarcastic remarks, the denial of any lingering feelings, the taunting laughter – something, *anything*.

But nothing.

My vision blurs, and I harshly scrub my eyes as the man is lifted to a stretcher and carried away. Just in time, Austin appears with another officer, both of them looking at the scene in confusion before looking at us. Austin moves to Cyrus's side, his shoulder bumping into mine.

"You good?" he says, his voice low and inquisitive.

I swallow hard, "Yeah."

"Unfortunately, you're all free to go," the officer grumbles. A quick glance at his name tag reveals the name *Aleks*. "If I were in charge, you four would be freezing your *asses* off in a nice and cozy eight-by-six."

Cyrus scoffs and says, "I'm guessing the only thing you're in charge of are the coffee orders, right?"

"Watch it, you little smart ass!" Aleks hiss. I catch Sibyl elbowing the teen's side, but all he does is roll his eyes.

"So, we're all good here?" she asks, her tone lifting towards the end as a bashful smile slips on her lips. The innocent act draws another scoff and snicker from Cyrus, earning him another elbow.

"Again; unfortunately. But you four listen closely," he takes a threatening step forward. His eyes harden as they drift over each of us before stopping on me. "I suggest you don't leave town. Who knows? Maybe some new evidence will come in. You folks have a good day."

With that, he turns on his heel and walks away.

"And there goes Officer Dipshit. Off to do the Lord's work one loitering teenager at a time," Cyrus says.

"C'mon, let's get out of here," Austin mutters.

****

The park looks a lot creepier given everything that happened. The crisp white snow glistens under the moonlight and is hypnotic in an ominous way, successfully keeping my attention. Warmth appears on my side, startling me for a second before I realize it's just Sibyl. Grunting draws my attention from her, and I watch as Cyrus keeps picking up ice-packed snowballs and pitching them against a tree.

His movements are aggressive and rhythmic, each hit getting harder and harder. Austin moves to the seat next to me and buries his face in his hands, a deep sigh leaving his lips. I look at him over before nudging his shoulder with mine. Slowly, his tired light brown eyes reveal themselves as heavy bags hang beneath them.

"Hey, things could've turned out worse," I try, but he just snorts.

"A shit ton of innocent people died, including my father and some officers just trying to do their job, a killer is after us, and your girlfriend, or whatever the fuck she was, was brutally murdered. I fail to see how this could've been worse.

I grit my teeth at the reminder and try to continue, "Well, for one, we're not locked up. I might be the town's resident psycho, but you guys have a pretty good rep. Maybe that can take some heat from us about the whole thing."

"Tell me about it! I don't think I can rock the serial killer look; well… I mean, maybe a really hot cult leader. I can totally see that happening," Sibyl says, her voice trailing off. "Should I start a cult? Are those still a thing?"

"No, and yes; you're scary enough on your own, we don't need likeminded sheep following after you," Austin answers.

"Boo."

"Anyway, those reasons are enough to make this shit not worth it, regardless of how it turned out," Austin says, turning to me. "Besides, we just got lucky that the cops chasing us were all killed by the black dog and they couldn't place that on us."

"And the ones killed by Him?"

"My guess? Whatever DNA they found just didn't match up with ours."

Almost in sync, we slump back on the bench and sigh deeply. A dull pain radiates from behind my eyes and rubbing at them only makes it worse. A pain that almost overshadows the one surging through the arm in a sling.

Almost.

"Well, I don't care how we got to this point; I'm just glad that we're all here," Sibyl claims.

"Amen to that," I say, smiling at her which she returns quickly. However, it slips from her face soon enough. "What?"

"I just," she pauses and exhales softly. "I just wish that we could've protected Ms. Ashford, y'know? I feel like we totally brought her into this, and she got the crappy hand, holding the crap-covered cards, and I don't know, lost in a crappy way and it's just…"

"Crappy?"

"Exactly!" Her eyes tremble, and I notice her breathing getting heavier. "We dealt her that crap hand, and she's dead for it! That's on us. She didn't deserve that. She only got dragged into this because we were messing with something that was way over our heads."

She was already involved the moment she met you.

"You know," Sibyl says quietly, drawing my attention. She shifts her green eyes to mine, and I take in the red in her eyes, the tip of her nose, and the flush of her cheeks. Her bottom lip trembles before she smiles. "I-I know she came off as a bitch for the most part, but... the way she talked about you all the time? The way she always lit up whenever you were brought up? Those things don't just happen unless you really love someone, and she *really* did."

A weightlessness settles in my stomach as a numbness takes over my body, and a buzzing noise rings in my ear. I barely take notice of someone getting up and moving in front of me.

I know.

I know she did.

And I was too much of a fucking coward to do the right thing with her – *I'm still a fucking coward.*

What could've been? How would our lives have turned out if I wasn't so fucked in the head? If I had met her at a café or a library? If we had bonded over a book that she read, and I had only pretended to score a date? If I had managed to charm her for a first, second, and third date? That we got to the point in our relationship where I would introduce her to Darcy and

Arthur, and they would mercilessly embarrass me over childhood stories and pictures?

What could've been?

"We gotta go," a voice says above me. I look up and see Cyrus has stopped throwing shit at the tree and is now glaring down at us. Austin is by his side, and I notice the teen's bruised and bloodied knuckles. His bloodshot eyes set off the blank expression on his face. "That freak is still out there, and we need to get our shit together before we meet His ass again."

Sibyl and I share a look, and I know the same memories of His relentless pursuit and brutality flash through her mind as they do in mine. Austin must've noticed as he takes a step forward and has to be pulled back by Austin.

"What the fuck is with that look?"

"L-look, you guys only saw the aftermath of His violence, but we went face-to-face with the guy. A whole police force was *totally* annihilated by Him, and you think the four of us can do anything?" Sibyl asks. This time, Austin takes the lead.

"So, we do nothing? You two know that we're the only ones who know about Him and the only ones who have the *chance* at stopping Him. You two were crying over Isolde's death two fucking seconds ago, and yet you're okay with sitting on your asses and allowing more deaths like Isolde's?"

It doesn't even register in my mind that I'm moving until I'm shoving Austin back, causing him to stumble back. I swear all I can feel my body heating up as my blood boils under my skin at the sheer fucking *audacity* he has to bring her up like that. Like he knew a damn thing about her.

Austin slowly approaches me; Cyrus is now by his side and Sibyl is by mine.

"Guys, we never said that we were just going to ignore His existence; we know that we can't! But we also know that we can't fight Him. We know nothing about Him, or, at least, nothing that can actually hurt or stop Him. I mean, what are we going to do? Kill Him with His backstory?" Sibyl says, damn-near begging for them to understand.

"The thing is that we can! You think wars were won by going in blind? No information is too small when it comes to going against an opponent – everything can be used as a weapon. We learn where He comes from, who's around Him, where He lives, where He sleeps, where He eats, where He shits; I want to know everything!" Austin shouts, his eyes burning with either determination, hatred, or a terrible mix of both.

"We'll die trying," I tell him, and his eyes slowly lock onto mine.

"We could die either way. Might as well make it worth it."

Fuck.

Sibyl and I don't say anything else, but our answer is clear.

"Good," Cyrus spits.

"We're going to head back home, but we'll keep researching tomorrow. The cops are definitely gonna be investigating in the woods, so we should all stick to working out what we already got and anything else that might surround it," Austin explains. "And maybe even come with some theories about how Chance was let go. There's no way in Hell they would do that unless there's some hard proof that he didn't do it."

With that, they turn and walk away.

After they leave, Sibyl pulls me aside, her eyes as dodgy as her movements. Before I can say anything, she practically throws her pastel green phone in my hands, and I fumble with it for a bit.

"What-"

"Answer me honestly; what do you think His intentions are?"

All of this leaves me disorientated and kind of speechless.

"What do you mean by that?"

"Like, do you ever get this feeling that there's something more going on? Like- like- like that time you said He was trying to speak to you."

"And?" I grit out.

"And why would He waste His time? He could've taken you out no problem but He didn't. Why? Why let you live for a whole frigging year and still let you go even when He had you right in front of Him? He might be sadistic, but He's not stupid. You've been around Him more than anyone and all that happened is you got beat up a little bit. Does none of that seem really, really weird?"

Just as I'm about to tell her that this is a stretch, that she's out of her mind for even thinking that there's more to it than what it is, I realize that the words don't – *can't* – come out.

Which is completely fucking ridiculous considering I looked into His eyes and saw nothing humane in those depths. She's wrong, and there's nothing more to it.

"Chance, let me ask you another question. Do you know the reason why the FBI kept such a close eye on you?"

"Obviously because I was the sole survivor," I answer.

"Chance, there's something that I didn't bring up since Austin and Cyrus were going a little revenge crazy… after they questioned me at the station, I was able to take pictures of some files they were keeping from us."

A violent shudder wracks my body at the words, a deep feeling of dread filling me as I tense all over. Her pause and biting of her lower lip nearly send me into hysterics, and I tighten my grip on the phone in my hand.

"Hurry up and say what you need to say!"

"J-just… look at the picture I took. I don't think I can even say it aloud. The password is 0998."

My fingers try to type in the numbers but keep messing up. Finally, I managed to unlock it and get into the gallery. At first, I'm not too sure what I'm looking at until it registers that it's a couple of medical reports, but two stick out.

No fucking way. Is this some sick joke?

Right there in the last photo were DNA results from last year's and yesterday's incidents. They were from the same person, but the problem is…

They weren't an exact match with me but instead with an immediate family member. They were a match with Hawthorne.

****

The bright screen of my laptop flashes for a second, shaking me from my stupor as I stare at the forum. After the revelation, Sibyl asked if I wanted her to forward the pictures, and I don't know why. I mean, why the hell would I want anything that won't help with this case?

But I do wonder how they got Hawthorne's DNA. Did He plant it there in hopes of trailing everyone off His trail or is this another one of His mind games? Honestly, either one would surprise me. That sick fuck would do anything to make my life a living Hell.

The screen flashes again, and I look at it to see yet another post coming in.

When I came home, I immediately got on my computer, anonymously posted on a forum page by attaching an image of Him, typed out the body of text, and, after a minute of just staring at it, I hit submit.

9:30 turns to 11:20 to 3:00 and it's when the clock hits 8 a.m. that the screen changes and an influx of replies starts to pour in:

DaRealOne420: Duuude! Dis is so freaky! All hetero but I had a dream about him!

Its_Your_Gurl_Melly: OMFG I dreamt about him too!

DeLuLuLola: Wait all of us had the same dream???? Should we be concerned?

69wastakenso68: I saw him in sum woods by my house w/ a black dog

420virgin: When I saw him he was deadass dancing nd shit staring up the sky… chat confirm?

ScottyForgot2BeamMeUp: Lmao what bullshit is this??

WannaHearAScaryStory: I saw him! I think he's a vengeful spirit. Someone, most likely a ballroom teacher, who was killed tragically... I feel so sorry for him... humans are scary

xSamuraiForLifex: IDK this is sounding the Mothman sightings... everybody thinking they see the same thing, but it's more like mass hysteria

DashingThroughJumpScares: @xSamuraiForLifex man, this is NOTHING like Mothman!! This guy has been everywhere! My friend's mom's neighbor reported seeing him before he killed some chickens from their yard!

WhiteBoyWa$ted: @ScottyForgot2BeamMeUp no bull I saw him and he looked exactly like that. Only difference is he wasn't dancing or anything. I saw him when I went out for a night jog, and he chased me until I got to a friend's house. Scariest shit ever fr

Imjustherefortheclout: you guys keep talking like he's a spirit or something, but I'm pretty sure he's an alien

DamnYouFlanders: @WhiteBoyWa$ted you're talking bout him moving like like a cartoon right? And then stopping when you look at him? Man, op better be careful because whatever the fuck this guy is... it ain't human

More and more comments pour in, and it solidifies all of my beliefs.

1: He's not human and might be some kind of demon.

2: There's nothing remotely good about Him.

3: There's no way in Hell He's linked to Hawthorne.

And 4: I'm going to die fighting Him, but I'm damn sure gonna make sure I take Him with me.

Prologue

A soft noise is the first thing that I notice, and when I sit up, a bit too quickly, a bottle of Daniel's falls to the ground. The clinking is harsh in my ears, and I groan from the pain pounding behind my eyes.

When the sound happens again, I have to drag myself from the couch and make my way to the front door. I wait a few minutes, and the sound happens again. Gently grabbing the curtains, I slowly pull them back, allowing a sliver of light to filter through, and tilt my head just enough to peek through.

There, I see two small boys; the oldest looks around eight or nine while the youngest looks about five or six. The older one is wearing an oversized dark gray hoodie, black jeans, and muddied black boots, and the smaller boy is wearing an oversized off-white hoodie, light gray jeans, and muddied light brown boots. His tiny free hand is clutching the strap of a small, duck-yellow backpack.

Knock.
Knock.
Knock.

That was the sound was: these kids knocking.

I drop the curtain a bit when they shift, but they keep looking at the front door when the oldest knocks again.

Knock.
Knock.
Knock.

"Hello? We need help. Can you open up, please?"

Wait… are these the missing kids from the campsite?

Considering some of the stuff found at the scene, I seriously thought that one of the kids had to have been a girl, and definitely with both of them being older than the ones here. Plus, I was expecting… more trauma, I guess?

I don't know what I'm getting at, but something's just off about them.

Suddenly, the smallest boy looks up, and my breath catches when I notice his eyes are pitch black. They're like two small black holes; not a speck of light can penetrate them, and the only thing I can feel is an overwhelming sense of dread settling in the pit of my stomach.

He quickly averts his gaze, but I had already moved my hand from the knob.

"What do you want?" I call out to them.
"Help us, Mister," the oldest answers.

A low, whiny growl sounds and my mind instantly goes to the Black Dog. They must've heard the same thing as the knocks come more quickly yet remain at three intervals. Their soft pleas fill my ear, combating with the Dog's growls that get closer and closer.

My heart's pounding harder and harder as I look between the kids and the Dog, yet I can't bring myself to open the door.

What if this is a trap?

"Help us!"

What if they're working with the Grinning Man?

"He's going to get us!"

But what if they're running from Him, too?

"Please, Mister! He's almost here!"

The Dog's standing there, right in the distance, and his eyes gleam like rubies while his yellowed teeth bare forebodingly from his muzzle, the threat behind them clear. He's standing right at the tree line but is taking slow, calculative steps forward.

My mind continues racing before I finally grab the doorknob.

To anyone listening to this, please let this be the right choice.

www.ingramcontent.com/pod-product-compliance
Lightning Source LLC
Chambersburg PA
CBHW031752200726
48289CB00013B/864